snapshots

Senon's friend
Justine!

snapshots

jarlath gregory

SITRIC BOOKS

First published 2001 by
SITRIC BOOKS LTD
62–63 Sitric Road, Arbour Hill,
Dublin 7, Ireland

A CIP record for this title is available from
The British Library.

1 3 5 7 9 10 8 6 4 2

ISBN 1 903305 04 7

Set in Adobe Garamond with Eurostile display titling
Printed in Ireland by ColourBooks, Baldoyle, Dublin

snapshots

OISÍN

So I phoned Peter to make him come to Saturnz, which it seemed like he would never do. He's a bit pissed off because he didn't go to Derry with Conan for the weekend, his main objection probably being how much fun it would all genuinely be. Peter likes Conan (not *likes* likes Conan, too much guilt), so I tease him and point out how tall dark and handsome Conan really is, and all I get is – crushed little sigh – 'Really? Well, there, I never noticed.' So I tell him fuck off, the guy's gorgeous, and he's like, 'Don't do this – I don't – what's the point?' So I push him too far, cos he needs someone to kick him up the arse. He raises a million boring reasons why we can't go – *how* do we get back – *who's* there except Shena – *who's* gonna pay the taxi – yes, he's trying to provoke me into slamming the phone down in my usual fuck-off fashion. But he means it, he means every dull question, and I just say who cares, Mr Dad is at some wedding, he might be back in time and he mightn't almost die of some wine-induced ulcer perforation this time and if there is a fucking taxi it'll not be too expensive and just go!

His motto, I work out at this stage, is 'Just Don't Do It'. I give off bad brain vibes and he says – crumble – 'Are you angry now?' to which I calmly reply 'Yes', and he says, 'OK, bye. Don't slam the phone! No, do, then I won't feel so guilty', and I assure him that I know right well he's not feeling one teeny-tiny-size-of-your-dick bit guilty, and put down the phone relatively gently, I hope.

Honestly, Peter is going to drive me to drugs. I mean it's not something we do. People still don't, pretty much. Not round here anyway. But all this worrying about *reality*. Maybe we should just get over it, lose ourselves to chemical irresponsibility.

In any case, I refused to let him sit at home and be miserable, or content, or whatever he was. The love of his life/existence/random time-filling day-to-day preparation for death would probably be there and every other person I'd phoned or seen all day was away out. Except Mum, whose imaginary migraine prevented her show-stopping performances at the wedding. They've been worse since Seán left us. Not that it matters, she's away somewhere inside her complicated head all the time anyway, enjoying the unpredictability of modern life and trying to fit all the uncontrollable events of now into one simple life-instruction (she's still working on it) – so I phoned Peter. Again. With details of the taxi. He told me I was a bollox, we were all stupid, we were going to have a shit night.

When we got to Saturnz the queue was massive and that's when we started to walk. I think it was my idea, not that I'd any idea where I was walking to, just away from all that shiny expectation. Peter was the sensible head who knew directions and stuff, and believed we were prime candidates for a beating, and stayed well on the inside of the road. When we forgot about how we were walking away from our entire night's plans, the night I'd busted heads to set ourselves up for, that's when we began to talk again, properly.

There was a damp sort of darkness, and I think we went away from the main road to avoid everyone else. The conversation was hardly amazing, just the pitter-patter of well-balanced friends.

'You know he's gunna be there.'

'Shut up.'

'It's a good thing.'

'No.'

'You know you wanna see him.'

'No.'

'Peter. You're in love. And you want to see him.'

'And that'll make it worse.'

I had to walk staring down at the dirt track to avoid all the cow shit under our feet. 'Yeah, I know.'

Despite the chill, or maybe because of it, it was kind of cosy just lumbering along in the dark. The sky was marbled in cloud with a moon whose drained, scum water light didn't reach earth.

We've had conversations before where we've tried to understand the whole gay thing – the whole *why us* bit. People always ask, 'What makes someone gay?' They never ask what makes someone straight, that's the assumption that everybody would be if something horribly wrong hadn't happened somewhere along the allegedly precarious road through adolescence. I mean, I wish something precarious had happened once in a while, it might have livened things up. You get tired of living second-hand. Crossmaglen is, contrary to popular belief, a stagnant and dull place to live, unless you're endlessly interested in the minutiae of your every neighbour's equally yawn-filled existence. Anyone can provide you with anyone else's life history, as I'm sure Seán knew only too well – so how did he make it all seem so invigorating? Without bombs and bullets to chew over, the town would have collapsed of boredom, having survived the famine. Maybe death gives people something to live for.

Me and Peter never reach any conclusion, except it'd be wise not to label ourselves, keep our options open. Hence my meeting with Shena tonight – except by now, that looks unlikely.

It's all too dark for Peter. He gets nervous just from walking under trees, and tries to stand still and hide each time a car drives past. He holds his breath and imagines they're slowing down, imagines footsteps behind us at every turn in the road, which is proving more obscure the further we go. He gets reassured by the sight of sheep, which leads to many hilarious jokes on my part. We walk for ages and all I can remember is him being scared and me running on ahead, not seeing where I'm going, enjoying the anonymity of it all. I don't want to sound paranoid, but when you walk streets all day in a town where everyone knows your life, and when you feel on the edge, then it's good to lose yourself on purpose sometimes.

Peter didn't seem to appreciate it. He was least upset by it all when we passed dimly lit houses, mostly show-off bungalows set way up gravelled drives which didn't look friendly, but would be somewhere to run to when the psycho axe-killers chased us.

I think Peter does buy into the notion of a well-paid job, a city suit, a countryside haven, and I told him he'd probably marry and settle down before life caught up with him. He said no, quietly, and eventually told me that he'd 'told someone else', and I was like 'God! When?' and when he said a couple of months ago I couldn't believe he hadn't told me before. He almost didn't tell me now, and he shut up for a whole five minutes when we passed a dumb bunch of trendies on a carry-out, halfway through the woods, in a picnic area or something. Peter seemed to think it was an IRA arms deal. I said if we just kept walking no one would care and he said *ssshhh* and trailed behind a little, looking clammy. I could just make out his face because it reflected the cars' headlights. It made him look luminous and ill, which he possibly is in reality. Peter may have found some pissed blokes as threatening as a pack of political killers, but once I brought him round to the subject for about the fifth time he tumbled out his story, glad to have his mind taken from the sinister surroundings and supplanted in the past. Or maybe I'm just making that up, but I'm just telling you the way I see him – safety first.

I tried to guess who he'd come out to, thinking of teachers because so many of them are nosy/concerned, only too willing to pep-talk you into popularity, obedience and the endeavour to do one's best, while throwing in a practical crash course in buggery too. But he said it wasn't a teacher, and I said, 'Not Tony?' Because Tony's this lovely wee bloke (not that I know him) who told Peter that he 'just wants cuddles'. Sweet, but no, which is a shame cos they'd make a great couple, I reckon. If they ever let themselves. And then he said 'A doctor' and I choked, and he said 'A stand-in doctor for mine', and then came the story.

So Peter had had this sore throat for a long time, and phlegm, the guy's obviously been coughing up his spleen for months. And he goes to the doctor, who gives him this cursory examination and then leans back in his chair, all casual, and says 'Strange question – are you heterosexual, homosexual or bisexual?' and Peter just says 'Homosexual' and dies. I mean, he just died. He sat there all dazed, and everything went fuzzy – I know exactly what he means – inside his head everything was buzzing, but the real world, in the doctor's room, was going in slow motion. He could only hear bits and pieces, through the word 'homosexual' echoing in his brain. Just couldn't believe he'd said it, out loud, to some stranger and then, the gist of what the doctor was saying was: because you are homosexual, you might have a throat infection. He had to explain thrush. Peter didn't understand why any of this was relevant – just cos I'm homosexual I get throat infections? – but he didn't say anything, you know? Couldn't probably. Still reeling. So this doctor stopped rambling at some point, and asked Peter if he was OK, and I swear to God he'd have looked pickled at this stage, as he does when he's flustered. He runs his hands over his face and looks gay. It seems everybody else sees this as his one personality trait, but in a good way, so everybody likes him. So Peter lies and says he's OK, gets his pills (as if he hasn't got a huge house-wifey collection already) and then the doctor asks him if he's actually had a sexual partner in the last, oh, four or five months? And Peter can definitely say no, but he's hardly going to say 'I'm a virgin and now I understand that what you've been driving at is a load of ugly bollocks', just takes his pills, nods a bit, and spends the rest of the day dithering. Thought about phoning me (and I would fucking well hope so) but doesn't because he'd hate to get het up over nothing, allegedly, though we've all seen that plenty.

So I'm stupefied, and have to admit it's a great story, and we stop at a bridge to catch our breath, catch up with our brains.

'But the thing is, you said it. I mean – does that mean you've – like – admitted it now?'

'Well –'

'Well, no, I know, admit is a stupid word, it's just – well, you never said –'

'Exactly! I always –'

'Yeah, always, like, reserved the right to – I mean, you always might've turned round and been straight.'

'Right.'

'So?'

The bridge was one of those old-fashioned ones made from lumps of rock that look all accidentally assembled but must have been carefully arranged to stay still for so long. This one must have started to crumble recently, because there were cement sections, conspicuously neat against the rugged and weed-tangled original. Peter threw in some stick he'd been peeling and crossed the bridge to watch it emerge, and disappear, somewhere, into the dappled river.

'So?' I prompted, and joined him to stare at the water, which soon got boring, and I began to rip at the weeds instead. They were delicate, not like you'd expect weeds to be, and came apart easily between my fingers. I chucked them back to the grass. Peter took his time answering. Or not answering. In the end I answered for him.

'It feels right, saying you're gay, and it's a relief, but it ties you down. It's like there's no going back, even if you want to. And you're not coming out.'

Peter gave one of his sighs, which he does so well, and agreed with a too-loud 'Yeah', as if he was being over-optimistic in reaching a conclusion. But I was more or less right.

'Because how do I know? You can't know.'

'You can't know who you'll fall in love with next.'

'It could be a girl. Not that I desperately need it to be – it just – might be.'

'So it's stupid to go to all the fuss –'

'Yeah, and then have to backtrack.'

'So we just – carry on?' Which somehow sounded a really depressing thing to say.

We could have walked to Dundalk to meet Louise and Kev leaving the cinema. Peter objected because it would mean leaving Dad stranded waiting for us at Saturnz, and we began to count time and wonder if Saturnz was worth trailing back for at all. There was Shena to consider – I told Peter that she was the reason I'd insisted on dragging him this far in the first place. He made the reasonable point: why was I walking away? And we began to walk back again, through the main road, which was more reassuring for Peter though I can't think why. I told him my plan was to sink five tequilas and ask her out again. He thought it was a very stupid idea, told me Shena was a bitch so why would I, then admitted that he could see why I would.

Shena is the one girlfriend I've ever had. I regretted never kissing her properly, I regretted asking her out, I regretted dumping her too. She's bad news, and I can't get enough. It's like we've become too mixed up with each other to ever let go, but at the same time we never know what we're supposed to be to each other. We flirt, and she says I'm ugly and I say she's gorgeous, but it's a relief to hang the phone up on her too. She wears people out.

I would ask Shena back again and mean it because she's never boring. I've become tired of sitting around obsessing over blokes who, no matter how many glances they send me, are basically too boring not to be straight. All the same, it was inevitable Peter would ask me: 'What about Jude?'

Jude is a very normal non-individual – bordering on pretty/handsome, toned and clean, statuesque – he's easy not to notice, likes to blend in but tends to get shoved to the side by his 'friends'.

The first time I met Jude, at least the first time I noticed him,

I was sitting on my own on the bus home from school, Peter having pissed off somewhere with his acting crowd, no doubt. Jude must have been sitting somewhere behind me. Just after the bus pulled off he stumbled into the seat beside me, just sat there, looking straight ahead. I think I looked around a bit sniffily for about half a second, then went back to gazing down the subway as if something interesting would emerge. As if it wasn't full of tarty schoolgirls and guys unfolding their urinating skills. As if I wasn't wondering what this solid, unmoving weirdo was doing in my seat.

When we stopped at the first set of traffic lights, he said 'Well, Oisín'. I sort of looked at him sideways, but he was still looking ahead, and that's when I realized he was beautiful. I wanted to sculpt his head that instant, feel those unpolluted planes glide into place beneath my hands. Maybe I fell in love with a perfect profile right then as the lights turned green, maybe I was curious as to why he even bothered being there, I'm sure I was still suspicious. But I was hooked. I said 'Well' and looked out the window again, suddenly aware of how ridiculous it felt to be behind glass, encased in plastic, chugging through a sun-stained town that flaunted its commerce, its filthy streets, all the insignificant people floating along that alimentary canal. It felt like we were the only two silent boys on the whole chattering bus, but the only two with anything worth saying. That sounds dumb, I know, but my brain was going crazy trying to break into his. Then he said 'How's the girlfriend Shena?' and I knew — well, I didn't know anything, as such, but how weird is it when someone you don't know starts asking about your private life? It made the whole scene less casual, more intimate and calculated; too huge a leap to say he's in love, but I made it anyway. I didn't feel like the biggest freak on the bus any more, but I guess I can't tell now how much he knew, how much he cared, how much he was even interested. But at the time – for fuck's sake, if he'd just been ugly I'd have ripped him to shreds on the spot. As it was, I played back at him, but kept withdrawn. Asked him what did he know about Shena? He said everything, and described her, and I said Shena was just fine and we weren't going out, by the way.

For some reason, I took my wallet out later, giving me something to do with my hands maybe, and he stole the fold-up address book that I kept tucked up in it. He read all the names and all, saying that now he knew I was into Greenpeace and Amnesty International, which he seemed to find satisfying and mystifying at the same time. In between him talking spooky shit, I was just looking out that window, ignoring our beautiful countryside and thinking how scary and exciting this idiot was.

I think the last thing he said was how he'd like to beat the shit out of one of the first-years. One of the loud girly ones. Obviously. This guy wasn't too stable, but I've loved him ever since.

So I said to Peter how I didn't expect to see Jude anyway, but we could always hang about for a while just in case.

We saw rows of lights ahead and Peter got all fidgety about what we would tell the Gardaí if they asked us where we were going (as if the Gardaí care about anything this late at night except their triple-overtime on cross-border duties). I said tell the truth, which bothered him for a change, he thought it looked suss us being together. So I told him he looked great in this artificial light and we all felt a bit awkward, us and the Garda man; kind of watching each other warily as we approached him, as if someone planned an ambush.

By now I felt a bit sick, walking all these miles on nothing to eat except a banana and the notorious tales of Peter. We were close enough to Saturnz and its nutritious fast-food trailers so that I didn't collapse or anything. We walked past Stars, where a few 14-year-olds who hadn't even made the grade for the over-16 alcohol-free rave zone were hanging around, pretending just to hang. We phoned home. Dad said he'd pick us up, not that we'd appreciate it.

I had all the tequila money in my pocket and nothing to show for it, so I went to the nearest horrible van-chippy thing and waited to order behind the lightweight pissed blokes who made me feel too old and glad I hadn't gone in the disco. Then Jude and two of his boring mates joined the queue.

Fuck!

I nearly talked to him. Instead I just looked at Peter, who was laughing merrily on a kerb, out of earshot but near enough to spot Jude in his trendy/ugly lime green shirt (fruity in a TopMan sort of way, so it doesn't count).

So I ordered, and waited for ages for change of a twenty, and stole surreptitious glances behind me. We locked eyes twice, not for long because I broke it. I always break it, I always look down. It would have been more natural to speak for fuck's sake, we're on speaking terms and all, but when he's with those check shirts he never speaks anyway.

I didn't feel hungry by the time I got back to Peter. I bit off a chunk of the chicken's carcass. Peter was like, 'Jesus, he was at Stars', and I threw a tough and gristly bit at him, and told him The Progress So Far while he wiped at his shoulder in case he got vaguely smelly or stained, as if anyone cared. Then we told each other how sad I was, and would have followed him except we lost him somewhere at the other trailer, where they'd stopped for no reason.

We went to look for Shena (as if), Peter finding a niche in the railings by the Saturnz door, which was already thronged with sweaty T-shirts, bruised heels, kisses, catcalls, put-downs, happy greetings, sad farewells, dozens of bad haircuts, and last-minute make-or-break appraisals now the erratic flattery of disco lights was left behind.

I was looking for Shena, I swear, but I kept catching Jude's gaze instead. He was perched on a back railing, set higher up and facing the door. He had the best view if he was looking for any-one leaving, but he was still looking at me.

Pathetic, isn't it? Either of us could have said hello, or ignored each other, and who would care? For all I know, he wouldn't, we all know how to misread people if we want to. My stomach had turned full circle by now and the food was making me ill and I threw the rest of the chicken burger over the railings. Some day I'll start a conversation, we've never had a proper one. If I can make something beautiful then I won't feel quite so worthless.

Until the next time when I can't bring myself to wrestle with his features, clean my head.

After ages of looking and bits of catching up and pretending to be friendly and no Shena, I gave up the act and went to the back railings, where I had a better view after all and sat with two of the boring blokes between me and Jude. But it made me feel I was doing something along the right lines, and Peter gave me a why-bother glance.

Shena was one of the last five people leaving, not because she had to be, no doubt she designed it that way so she could say it later at the top of her voice. She was with some ugly bloke, greasy long hair, predictably, because anyone who looks out of place suits her fine.

We did talk and all, a bit, this guy she was with kept saying 'You gotta be in my band!' and she kept saying 'I have no rhythm! I can't sing! Oisín, tell him I have no rhythm!' and it's true, she doesn't, and I said so, and kept looking over my shoulder, and she was like, 'Oisín, yeah, be with you now – hey, were you inside?' so I said no, and she looked puzzled, but shrugged it off for the pleasures of yon boy's long tongue, and I saw that by now Peter was blathering with someone and a friend of theirs was with Jude and they were all standing in a corner. By the time I said a goodbye to Shena that she didn't hear and squeezed through to the railings again, Jude had hopped over and gone.

Peter was all, 'Hard luck – so what did you expect?' and we trailed over to the carpark across the road, dodging traffic and feeling a bit tragic, like something important should have happened.

Peter said, 'At least you still have your money', and asked what about Shena's man, who he should have known but didn't. I told him how she'd said 'Peter, for God's sake, does he ever get a woman', and how I'd said 'Well, did it ever occur to you that maybe he doesn't want one?' and she'd been all knowing smiles and went back to Mr Guitar-for-a-dick, who probably sits in a pool of aural wank all day and what's so special about that?

So Dad was there all right, waiting like a good dad does because I haven't learned to drive yet since Seán escaped into the sunset.

Jude was standing about with a group of no-ones waiting to get into this jeep. Typically, he got in last and they drove ahead of us. We kept staring at each other through the glass until the jeep sped off and left us behind, struggling to get through the crowds at the chip vans.

SNAPSHOT

The dog always sat in the same place, at the same ramshackle wall, watching everybody else's business. Cars and people, people and bikes, other dogs and more cars. Occasionally, the other dogs barked or sniffed, or the cars smelled nice. A lot of people wore green, with hard hats and big guns. They had black smeared on their faces and walked with a casual uneasiness, their eyes wary. The black and green was for camouflage so they couldn't be seen walking the grey, scarred streets of Crossmaglen: mostly, it worked. They were no longer remarked upon when they paraded or stopped traffic. You could hear conversations drop when they walked past, though.

Jude always winks at the dog, who never winks back. The wall has been partly rebuilt, the bricks fresher and more sturdy at the entrance to the dump beyond. Jude still thinks of it as Humpty Dumpty's wall, but, on reflection, realizes that just because the egg smashed doesn't mean the wall collapsed. He can remember that when he was in playschool he always refused to

18

sing along to Humpty Dumpty, folding his arms, frowning, near to tears when the rhyme climaxed and the teacher cajoled him to join in. He'd never admitted it was because he didn't want Humpty to die.

Maybe he was bored, but today the dog followed. He's a terrier, he doesn't have a name that Jude knows of, he's a bit scabby but pleasantly ferocious looking. He bounds and growls a little as Jude scuffles home, the housing-estate of maze-like complexity, contradictory footpaths, back-to-back bathrooms, spidery drainpipes and not enough greenery. The soldiers are the greenest things in Cross, the houses are uniformly ugly, the play parks look like they fell out of the sky and never recovered.

Jude takes the key from under the mat and has to shoulder open the door because it balks at the carpet. Terrier comes in too, leaps upstairs behind him. Parents don't notice because they aren't there.

In the messy, musty bedroom where the windows are never opened, Jude drops his denim jacket in a corner. Terrier takes a tour of his new home.

The bed is colourful, if tired. The carpet has been smothered and is barely visible beneath rummaged piles of paper, used biros, scattered pencils, books, tapes, CDs, a couple of letters and lots of clothes, some new, mostly happily mismatched, all a bit smelly. The beige walls are covered in photos ripped from magazines. There are the usual suspects of pop tarts and movie magicians, tacked up and torn, a wealth of faded glamour. Terrier likes what he sees, enjoys the stuff and stink.

Jude rolls over the bed and sticks on a DJ remix tape that he borrowed from a friend. It suits his dumb mood. He squeezes into the windowsill where he has a view of concrete geometry – 'dum *dum*my dummy dum dum dum dum *dum*my dummy dum dum' – and tosses terrier a half-eaten biscuit. It is ignored. Dreams evolve in the room where new cultures could easily flourish unchecked. Terrier's incessant panting feeds an odd notion.

In the bathroom, Jude begins to strip like he's a filmstar. The white walls complement his tanned body, his scrawniness fits the confines of the steamed-up shower. He lets the water scald, caress and wash away his thoughts as terrier splashes beside him, yelping, whingeing, turning yellow as Jude laughingly pisses over him. When the lather has gathered in the drain and Jude tingles, rubbing a hand over his stubbly head, he reaches for his razor.

Terrier tries to lick the shaving foam until he sees Jude slice it from his chest, round his taut neck and jaw, under his oxters and wrists. Scrape and flick, rinse and balance. Sparingly it is drawn from his belly up. His totem penis quivers, sniffing the air like the curious dog. Jude lowers his face and delicately cups his testicles, while terrier whines. The razor licks and blood slides gently from fingers to toes.

Jude allows his face to wince. He speaks to terrier for the first time. 'Not only women bleed,' he tells him, and terrier cocks his head in sympathy.

In his newly shaven state Jude walked the town. He kicked a plastic bottle past bungalows whose flower gardens gave the illusion of isolation. They were sat back from the road but the double glazing still shattered when bombs exploded. He and the bottle danced past the refurbished Rangers' Hall, where you could hear the cheers of football training. A helicopter circled overhead like a vulture waiting to swoop.

The Hall looked stately, the expensive iron fencing proudly encircling a pitch and grounds that tabloid libel had paid for. The barracks is still next door, but. It's huge.

Scuffy trainers were right for a superclean day like this. He could kick that bottle for miles, leave Cross behind, walk out into the world and never be found. The plastic clanged against metal rungs.

The barracks is something that's there every day. When Jude looked up to the top of the lookout post it was like he saw it for the first time.

A tower of galvanized steel that people threw paint on. It was smattered with yellow and white, quite striking against the green-black shell. Broken bottles lay in the space between the wall and grid. There were stories about some eejit climbing it with the tricolour. A symbolic gesture, he'd said. Symbollocks.

Taking a left he passed family homes, the family chemist, into a little industrial dumping ground across the road. There wasn't much need for an industrial dumping ground because there wasn't much industry. This left plenty of space for the oil cans, rusted jaws of dead mechanics, lazy and debilitated efforts which gave local plant life something to fight for. An ancient JCB loomed like a dinosaur.

There was fuck-all to do, no one to impress. Maybe it was time to feed the dog, or something, maybe the dog would expect it off him now. Jude turned heel to home and wondered if it had shat all over the place in his absence.

The dog was out of sight but the telephone was ringing. Jude snatched it up, wondering who the fuck –

'Hello?'

'Hello – is that Jude?'

'Yeah.'

'How are ya?'

'Who's this?'

'This is Oisín Grant.'

'Aw – Oisín – hello.'

'How are ya?'

'Fine'.

'Good. Keeping well?'

'Yeah.'

'Great.'

'Er –'

'Are you still OK?'

'Yeah, yeah, grand.'

'You're supposed to ask how I am.'

'Yeah – are you OK?'

'Yeah, great.'

'So – eh.'

'I'm phoning to ask you a favour.'

'Oh.'

'I want to take your photo?'

'– right –'

'I'm planning this brilliant sculpture, and it's gunna be you and you have to say you will.'

'I – eh – I dunno.'

'Ach, no, you have to. Because I have it all planned and I stole the scrap and everything.'

'Scrap?'

'It's gunna be in scrap.'

'Me in scrap?'

'Yeah, ya lucky thing.'

'Um –'

'All you have to do is say you'll sit for some photos, or a drawing or two, it'll not take any time at all.'

'Well, where would it be?'

'Well, wherever. Belfast maybe. I'm in Belfast at Queen's.'

'Yeah, how's that?'

'Salright. It'll be better if you come and do a photoshoot. Will you come?'

'I'd love to,' Jude said, and they both nearly died of surprise.

OISÍN

So much has happened. Let's go back to when Jude agreed to come visit me for a photoshoot.

We agreed that I would meet him at the train station in Belfast. For a week the idea was all that occupied my thoughts. I had, of course, each moment planned, just because you always do. I knew what I would say, and the shapes he would assume in answering my words. I didn't need to think he loved me, I just needed to think that he might. If at any time he told me outright that he didn't, that would be OK. We could put ourselves behind the denials, I would drop my drawing pencil and never have to see him anymore. It would be simple except I can never let go of the hope, or belief, that he still loves me back. I've always believed that, and need to see it through.

I couldn't wait, in the end, to meet him in Belfast. I got Dad to drop me off at the train station, he has his uses.

I stood on the platform and shivered. As always, all of us waiting for a train shuffled from foot to foot, catching each other's eyes, never speaking. I don't remember any of their faces. I dare say we all could have got on well – who wouldn't be intrigued by a stranger striking up conversations? Doesn't happen much. I reread the billboards on the opposite wall. I replayed the Valentine's card I had sent Jude, over and over through my memory, searching its words for giveaway signs. I'm sure I could remember what I'd written if I had to, but by now I've mostly blanked it out. One phrase still rings very true – *I love your bad temper and your sad smile.*

Apparently Jude has an evil temper. I've never seen it myself, but I get the idea. He does bunch up those fists like he's bitching for a fight. He was in the paper once for karate champion, or something like that. A suitable way of venting anger. Peter told me before that he'd put his fist through a wall in school. Not brick, one of them plasterboard ones in the mobile huts that are used to ease overcrowded classes. There was a really stupid reason why he'd done that. I don't know, he'd broken his ruler, I think. Something anal like that.

Peter had overheard them on the school bus, picking Jude's Valentine's card apart. He had to prepare me for the shock that my name had come up.

Once all the lads had passed it around and read the 'disgusting' bits (I meant every word), they'd inevitably taxed their little brains on the puzzle of who'd sent it. Apparently, the writing gave it away and it was 'too like poetry to be anyone except Oisín Grant'. I mean, I'd made the writing crap on purpose. And it wasn't poetry, it was just real.

I suppose I can't slag them off for being right, though. In a way I was glad they knew. Jude was meant to know who it was from. If I meet his friends in a shop or anything, they always give me looks that show surprise that I belong in the real world too. It's fucking great. 'Oh my god, there's that queer! He's shopping! Ugh!'

He arrived with minutes to spare, a Nike bag slung over one shoulder. He was a mismatch of labels, as usual. I didn't know whether to hate his buying them all, or admire how he didn't buy into one.

'Well.'

'Well.'

'I wasn't meant to be here, but it turned out to be handier in the end.'

'Right.'

He didn't look overjoyed to see me.

So the train journey was a laugh, or maybe not. We had to stand in the corridor and imagine all the scenery on fast forward, fleeting through our field of vision, dancing backwards into oblivion. We were stuck between a toilet and the kitchens. Jude smiled at the pretty women in uniform. At least the journey wasn't long. We couldn't have exhausted conversation because it really wasn't the place for it, squishing oneself up against tool cupboards to let fat businessmen in for a piss, or let a waiter past with his plate full of salad that looked like he dribbled on it.

Belfast is nothing special, so we didn't bother with being over-awed when we stepped off the train. It's a horrible place. Very open and somehow with a derelict feel – nightclubs all close early, that doesn't help much. Before we went out, we had to pretend to be friends. My flat is a mess and I didn't care. Jude had a bit of a nosy round the bedroom, studied my drawings that held the walls in place. They were of him.

'Is it weird seeing yourself on the wall?'

'Hmmm', as if to say, no. 'There's a wild lot of detail,' he said. I mean, I would hope so. His head's split open like a crocus and his face is bruised, bony and leaking blood. More of a death mask than a face. I still needed more. I wondered if he'd mind posing naked. I could decimate him.

I wore my eyeliner. 'You look like some sort of queer,' he said with a wrinkled nose.

'Queer is cool.'

'No it isn't,' he said, but more to himself. I made him a fake ID before we went. He was wearing that horrible shirt again, but apart from that he looked old enough. He looked me up and down before we left, and kindly deferred judgment.

'Why do you wear stuff like that?' Jude asked huffily.

'Like what? It's normal.'

'You're not normal.'

'I'm – pretty normal.'

'You're not pretty either,' he said, slouching ahead, letting his laces trail behind him. He flung the insult over his shoulder.

'You just want to be different,' he said.

'Well you just want to be the same!' I called, but he ignored me.

We all met up in Xerox. Peter was there, drinking a daring vodka and pure orange juice. He gave me a saucy wink when I sauntered in with Jude. Roo was sitting in her gothic splendour, with her customary pint. She was in the middle of explaining something very important to Peter, no doubt concerning her boyfriend back home and the mess she'd be in when he discovered she'd been shagging some metalhead in Belfast. She immediately lit on Jude – 'I've heard so much about you! No, really!' – and Peter had time to whisper 'I never thought he'd arrive' before I went to buy the first round.

None of this matters. Who cares what boring people I met, or which ex-classmates I tried to ignore all night? The point is, the crowd was very straight. I chatted to Peter and our other sundry friends much like any other night. Jenny was sparkling. Sinéad was scatty. Clare drank soda water and lime. We weren't making the usual group effort, just trying to find something that Jude could comfortably talk about. It turned out that Sinéad had shifted some bloke in his class and it had all been terribly embarrassing. Roo wasn't drinking enough, she must have been poor that week. I would have bought Jude pints, if he'd let me, but he was being boring and careful and safe. Roo drank them instead, and teetered merrily round for another dull night. She had great fun slapping me across the face when I accidentally stood on her traily black skirt. Jude was a tad horrified, despite his own alleged inclination for violence.

'Don't mind her,' I said. 'She's sober.'

What can I say? We danced a bit. Jude was surprisingly not

bad, for a lad. Roo wasn't apologetic, but stayed around and was almost friendly in an attempt to see if 'we' were leading anywhere.

Belfast nightclubs depress me. When the lights go up on the sweaty faces, shifting couples are flushed out, the trash is swept before you leave the dancefloor – then I feel a bit more sad for us all.

I looked around the crowd. At least when I wake up in the morning I'll be intelligent, I thought. They won't.

Back home, it all felt wrong. Jude undressed and proved to be smooth. He insisted on taking my bed, so I had the sleeping bag, lay at his feet. He paraded a little in his ill-fitting Y-fronts. We looked across the rooftops from my damp and cloudy window. Our breath mingled and trickled down the glass. He didn't have a lot to say.

In the dark, it felt like the walls crawled with spiders and nightmares boiled in his brain. He was restless. Any time he spoke, his words were in trouble, tripping over those lips. Slips of the tongue, dripping, licking the spittle-flecked phrases up at a distance – slow and misplaced.

Between the cracks of society. Alone and lucky. Side by side in a dark bed, moonlight painting our backs with a sweet, subtle sorrow. Just glad to have known someone who – or maybe I just dreamt that bit.

I woke up in the middle of the night, the creak of the floorboards under my back magnified by the silence that threatened to blind us, carry us away. I remembered how it felt to be four again, the smell of dust conjuring monsters up from under the bed, their quick fingers grappling with bedsheets, their minds and eyes focused on mine as I would jolt upright and scream for life.

The sleeping bag was twisted somehow round my legs; the zip bit my shoulder. My last dream shone in my head.

I'd been standing doing some mundane task at the kitchen table. Then I felt my head explode, I could see the white light radiate, tinged with navy at the edges. I thought I'd died. It hurt.

As my pulse rate decelerated I unbunched my fists and spread out my arms to get my bearings. Something in the air, or a lack of something, told me Jude was gone.

I raised myself up on an elbow and saw the empty husk of the bed, didn't stop to think. I pulled on my jeans, the shirt with only two buttons left and a pair of trainers. I stood on a pile of CDs, didn't care, checked the flat but knew he wasn't there.

Somehow it was brighter than I would have thought. Beauty hovered on the ordinary things. A glimpse of sofa through the crooked doorway, the damp patch in the hall, a stray gleam of moonlight I could trace down the banister, into the corridor.

I locked myself out of the flat. I didn't realize til I went to the door three floors down and couldn't get out.

So of course Jude had taken the keys, he was gone. I stood like a bollox wondering where to run.

The rest of the house, I discovered, was silent – save for the dead drunk snores from the ground-floor flat. The remains of a party littered their bit of hall, the door was wide enough open to walk in and see the ugly faces, as slack-jawed in sleep as they are during daytime.

Back on the third floor I was faced with the window, tried to heave it open. It led to a six-foot drop and a garage roof, but was taped shut with silver foil – to stop the draught, or suicide students.

I stared dumbly at the door for a while, dunno what for, wondered if Jude was ever coming home – wrong phrase; you know what I mean.

The kitchen was open, I stole a knife and tried to break back in the flat. As if. This guy showed me how to do it once, he'd held back the wall, I swear, he jiggled the lock about until the door swung open and nearly took off his arm. It was no good, I couldn't. So I used the knife to slit open the seal on the window.

I perched myself on the edge of the windowsill, watching my trainers dangle over the garage roof. The window overlooks a used-car lot that has an air of expectancy when darkness descends, like all the cars are dreaming of escape. The freer cars moved lazily along the streets. Ambulances too, they're a constant round here. I let myself fall, thinking I was in good company if I shattered all my bones. When I realized I'd survived it occurred to me that I couldn't turn back.

So what?

I had to get to the yard. I levered myself down between the next garage roof and the gutter that was full of shitty moss. It tumbled down on top of me when I spilled it. Part of it came away in my hand.

With dirt in my hair and streaks down my jeans, I wondered for the first time where Jude had gone. Did I look desperate? And were there policemen ready to catch me when I fell through the roof? I was standing on this metal yoke – dunno what it might have been, a frame or something that was rusty. It didn't collapse. I was lucky enough, it shook and echoed as I sprang off it, down on my hunkers in the concrete garden.

I discovered the gate was padlocked on the outside. It's corrugated steel, set in a corrugated steel fence that's seven foot high and topped with barbed wire. There's a me-sized gap that had to do. I was amazed to find a ladder bedded in a corner. It turned out to be too long. I had to set it halfway down the yard, in the middle of someone's washing that had fallen into dust. Beside the bunker that's empty and covered in plastic. Below the frosted window, much too high and narrow to let light through. Everything looked like *Batman*. The ladder kept slipping cos I had to crawl up it. It was at such an angle, but didn't slide away. I had to clutch at the sides of the hole and throw myself through, bang in front of those wounded cars. My glasses nearly fell off, but I caught them, being in top form that night.

I went walking. I followed the normal way into town. There are always little piss rivers leaking out of smelly drunks. They give you tired looks and try to raise one hand, all they can manage. I stomp on, all this anger sending me mad, and I wonder if Jude'll be impressed when I tell him. He must be moping. I stroll past a gang of tracksuits at the bus stop. It's more of a mausoleum for the aforementioned dropouts. Turning the corner I can see him up ahead, drinking something through a straw outside the BP. Apparently BP are bastards in the Third World, so I heard. It never stops anyone buying things there at stupid times of the morning. In Mopey World.

I leg it over. He looks at me shifty-eyed but says nothing. He doesn't look different, I mean, he doesn't change his expression – just sits there as if I'm meant to explain myself. The wall is low and I'm taller for as long as I decide to stand. I sit and swing my legs instead.

He's wearing scoby clothes cos he doesn't give a fuck. And then I say, 'I got out the third-floor window.' He doesn't stop sucking on that straw, he's drinking milk. Looking at the ground and scabbing up some grass that pokes out of a crack in the tarmac. But he nearly smirks, then lets his shoulders droop a bit further. Shifts how he sits til he's cross-legged and goes, 'Shouldn't have bothered.' And that annoys me. That annoys me and I go, 'I was worried, asshole.' And he goes, 'I'm not your asshole,' and I start to feel a trickle of sweat slide from my oxter to my ribcage. I don't know what to do. Go for broke? Because everything is leaking now, as it does when things happen without your control. At the time, the best and worst things have a protective inevitability. Everyone has these moments when there's no time to be scared.

I remember the unreal glow of the BP in tricolour – and the swooping ambulance that maybe was taking some poor thing to hospital. Or was maybe too late. Maybe. And I thought if I lived to be eighty, and sick, and dying, I'd have hated not to try or

even let him know. I mean, he knew, the cunt, I bet he did. He
started it, after all. But right then I knew he could end it all too.
It made me mad as fuck to think he'd make it look he fucked me
over —

But I'm running away with myself, as I do. I spat over the
kerb with him. He didn't move; he mightn't have been breathing.
Maybe the two of us were trying to pretend like our breathing
wasn't accelerated. Like we weren't anxious sexy queers. Like his
profile wasn't killing me. I can never see his face without wanting to trace those lines under my fingers. His face makes me
believe in God.

I remember every detail much too clearly. I sicken myself, he
makes everything around him assume a clarity and significance.

'Jude.'

'Hmm.'

'I have something to ask you.'

Sharp breath. 'Hmmm.'

'About that card.'

'Card?'

'The Valentine's card you got.'

'Did you send it?'

'I heard you thought that! What was it like?'

'Dunno.'

'Don't be stupid, like you don't remember. Or did you get
loads?'

'No.'

'So?'

'What?'

'What was it like? I heard it was poetry.'

'Sort of. Weird.'

'And you thought it was me?'

'Did you send it?'

He was looking in the opposite direction. I was tired of his dumb-fuck act.

'Do you think I'm madly in love with you?'

He laughed. Nervously. All the little particles of air around us shattered.

'Well, I didn't,' I said.

Pause. 'Aw.'

'Did you like it?'

'Och, I dunno.'

'Yeah, you know.'

'Don't remember,' he said, and stood up. He crushed the milk carton in one of his oversized, scabbed-up hands. A thin trickle of milk crept down his thumb. Leakages were everywhere.

I didn't know what to feel when he left. He left me feeling smaller on the service station wall, loped off out of sight. Not that I was looking. I wasn't.

I waited for – it might have been hours. For all I cared. I mean, it wasn't – but you know. Just sitting, like, not knowing how to react.

A car pulled into the station. It didn't make much noise. As it slithered off the other way I unfolded myself, took one more deep breath. The petrol was rank but at least it was real. Several sad cars bled on the roadside, rainbows died and trickled down the drain.

Jude was waiting by the front door, grinning with the keys. We didn't speak a word on our way back up the stairs.

I slept badly, until Jude snapped back the curtain and gazed on a Belfast morning. I'd been drifting, waiting for him to stumble out of bed. I watched him dress, him quick and me lazy, before I crawled into the bed and snuggled up in his second-hand heat.

'That's me up for the day,' he said, and I closed my eyes and murmured good morning. I remembered last night as the worst of my life and fell asleep.

I couldn't lie still for long. When I woke an hour later, I threw back the covers and swung my legs over the edge, found the filthy carpet underfoot, stood up and tousled my hair in the yolky sunlight. I was still there in the mirror where I'd been the day before, which was reassuring. I looked at myself for a while, skinny and unshaven, decided I was fit to be seen. Dragged on combats. Couldn't find socks. Took a T-shirt for decency. Turned off my brain and followed the smell of burnt pig into the sitting room, where I found Jude propped in front of the TV with a plate of cholesterol on his knee.

'Tea in the pot,' he said without lifting his face from the flickering screen. 'Tea,' I replied. I spilled some over my hand when I poured it, but he either didn't notice or didn't care. I was too dead to stick it under the tap. I was nearly too dead to feel it, but that scorching sensation stays for days, drags you back into the real world when you find yourself wandering. I scratched at it while I supped the tea. He hadn't taken the best mug.

'Food.'

It wasn't a question. He held it out for me to take, a slimy fry on a cracked old plate. Greatest spread I've ever seen. He settled himself once more, hunched up over his mug. While the cathode rays slid through his eyes, I imagined Shena piled up in front of me. I made a little picture of her from the bacon and eggs, sausages and toast. I sliced her into little bits and ate her for breakfast.

'Hum,' I said between mouthfuls. 'What do you want to do?'

'Dunno.'

'Yeah you do.'

'Whatever,' Jude said, then stirred himself, shook himself out. 'Let's go shopping.'

So we did, sort of. We set off past the split-open window, Jude kicking the knife down the stairs, checking the post, laughing at the ladder where I'd left it in the yard. We dodged all the dog shit, walked through rollerbladers, made it to the usual places; me barging ahead and him trundling somewhere behind, most of the time, not forcing himself through the crowds.

We looked at lots of trash and didn't buy a thing. Maybe that's just as well, there's something very intimate about shopping together. I think I'd lost all hope in him by now. The freak wouldn't speak to me; I mean, I tried, I really did, I said stuff – it wasn't maybe fascinating, but he barely responded. Maybe I was trying too hard to be nice and normal. Maybe he was lost.

One thing I remember always makes me reconsider. On our way back to the flat we passed a black family, the two wee kids were holding hands, a boy and a girl, dressed up like Christmas presents. As they went past, Jude said, 'Aw. Cute.'

And I nearly collapsed.

We made it back in time to take a few snapshots. They were terrible. I wasn't in the mood anymore, I didn't try. He sat cross-legged, 'The Oisín pose', he said. That was cool too. We ran for the train, somehow it was fun. The last thing he said was, 'Remember how you got out the window?' and I said yeah, and he said, 'Well the key was in the back door.' That kills me, it cracks me up.

I was still relieved to see him get on that train with a clumsy wave, though. Let me get on with my life.

Now that Jude is gone I've tried to settle back into a normal routine, as if I've ever had one. There are tutorials to pretend to attend.

I've burnt toast and slept on the bus and spent a small fortune on Walkman batteries. When I'm at home, Mum and Dad just annoy me. Specifically, I feel annoyed by how reasonable they always are. If I'm grumpy, rude, untidy and distressed, they are, in return, perfectly lovely. They don't pry. They don't shout, snarl or ask what's wrong. They put up with me and ask about the good things in life, the things I barely notice are there – university, girlfriends, Peter and his woes. Maybe they just don't care, now that Seán's not around. They have little to do but preserve niceties.

Peter has buried himself in his pillow. He's no use at all. While I dream of schemes to recapture Jude, he urges me to be practical and to leave him behind. He says it's worked for him.

'It hasn't,' I said. 'You're still caught up in him.'

'Not as much,' Peter said, frowning, evaluating all the time he's wasted in fantasy.

'Wouldn't you rather do something? Tell him? Or try to hang out where he hangs out?'

'No.'

'You would.'

'Not in the long run.'

'In the long run,' I said, 'we're all dead anyway.'

So Peter is throwing himself into recreation. He's begun to save for the clothes he really wants. He's changing his diet and clearing his complexion. He's trying to change himself instead of changing events. Which is OK for him, I haven't the patience. I want Jude now.

Every day I lie in bed til the morning dulls and stains the curtains dark again. For three hours a week I attend necessary classes. Otherwise; I spend a lot of time drawing, colouring and painting my obsessions into lines and shapes that drag my thoughts across paper and hold them there forever, or at least until they begin to decay.

A big fuss was made of my coming home in the holidays. I

was expected to come home for Easter, I had no choice.
Although I would have been content to laze about Belfast, it was
apparently my duty to go home for Mass and stuff.

When they cover up Jesus for Easter you notice him for the first
time in ages. Everyone makes it to Mass, ordered rows of man
and wife, bored kids and the old people (getting scarcer) who
close their eyes and pray loudly. The purple shrouds give all those
anonymous statues a subtle kind of life, like strategic hoodlums
ready to break out of the shadows if your attention strays to, say,
the blond guy sitting four pews ahead who keeps looking over his
shoulder to catch Jude's eye. He is squashed up between his parents, in a navy tracksuit that doesn't bode well personality-wise
… Well, any Jesus could tell you buggers can't be choosers, not
in this place of peace, worship, and, one suspects, unrequited
love. I can't remember his name but I've seen his lovely face in
prayer books, probably. Or torturing cats by the roadside – it's
that sort of face. It slides upwards, smiles easily, too pale to be
wholesome. The kind of face Jude might smile back at shyly,
thinking *why me?*

The lack of drama at Mass is disappointing, considering that
we're there to plumb the depths of our souls and rejoice in the
preparation of a new life after death. What are we all going to do
with Eternity? Our minds balk at the notion and go for a dander
round the assembled talent instead. That's how their minds col-
lided, I suppose, traipsing around the chapel in search of a diver-

sion. They were cute. When they went up to kiss the cross, he stabbed Jude with a smile and squeezed into the queue in front of him. Jude had no choice but breathe in his dandruff, relish that ass. I'm sure he registered this appreciation.

A sudden marriage that; tiptoeing up the aisle together, kneeling for as close a kiss as was allowed, sloping back to their seats. They swapped one more glance before it was time to stand as one and proclaim our thanks to God that the rite was over.

So it looks like I've lost Jude to someone still at school. It turns out he's called Ciarán, he's fifteen, he's had a few girlfriends – and he reckons he's cool. So why should he make such an effort with Jude?

I've spent ages thinking about the time we had in Belfast. I had a chance, even just to say I liked him. We were on our own and no one else would have to know – even if he said no way, he'd hardly go running to his mates about it.

I realized why I couldn't go through with it. I couldn't even try to get close to Jude because of Seán. I could only think of when he went away, even though he knew how lonely I would be. And I couldn't help thinking it was all my fault that he did.

It was decided some days ago that all the school 'friends' had to meet once again.

What's the point of getting away from everyone if we're only going to throw ourselves together at every available break? Presumably we're all busy enough during the year, getting on just fine – or better – without the ghosts of the past to bore us all to tears. Then when we have free time, we all squeeze into the corner of a bar, just like we did in the Common Room, and have to reel out all the old insecurities, animosities, stories we've told five times before.

I still went, of course. Someone persuaded me it would be funny. I can't remember this night of tequila, I only know what I was told later by Roo, who wasn't there, and the boys who kindly took me home.

So some people flirted with other people. Some people put their college education to good use, and set about drinking pints. They complained about the price. The various demerits of trains and contraceptives, central heating and the war in Afghanistan were all discussed. I say 'they' but I mean 'we', I suppose. I suppose I joined in. I know I did, then, before I hit the tequila. In any case, we were there, in a corner by ourselves, as tumultuous teenagers passed us by.

The repetition of our lives startled me. I could remember being one of the GCSE people, wondering why university heads bothered coming back. They were always full of stories about how the rest of the world, outside this town, was great. I say 'they' but I mean 'we', I suppose.

Peter sat there being sensible, alcohol isn't part of his purification plan. He lives on brown rice and fruit these days. It was all we could do to force him from his house, but that's not important. Perhaps he hopes to sweat his homosexuality out through his pores.

I was listening to someone, David maybe, bore us all with his lurid women stories. I noticed that Declan had started smoking. He was sharing one with Deirdre, his arms around her shoulder. The high-backed chairs blocked my view, created a box of ill-fitting egos, vying for attention or dying for relief.

Peter nudged my elbow and nodded towards the toilet door. Jude was there, tucking in his shirt, slowly dissolving into the men who were chequering the bar. We swapped a look, me and Peter, and he gave a shrug as if to say *whatever*. Turning an ear back to conversations, I wondered what had we become? A class of clichés. Mark began every sentence with 'As a social scientist'. He's turned into a fucking essay. He thinks he understands the working class. At the same time, he disclaims being middle class (it's just that his parents are).

I stood up to leave, like anyone cared. I shouldered and elbowed my way to the bar, glancing into eyes that would hold for a second, before we roughly shoved a way through. Familiar faces glided, ducked and disappeared in choppy waves of sweat, glass and love-torn bodies. As I strained to see his shaven head, I saw Shena swanning her way around admiring boys. She spotted me, waved, smouldered over with outstretched arms. Tonight she was determined to be sociable and happy.

I bought her a tequila. I showed her how to salt her hand, it glittered like diamond dust against translucent skin. Her face grimaced in distaste as she poured back the shot, and a trickle of juice escaped her lips as she laughed and proclaimed tequila foul. She bought me one back. They were only a quid, no one manages many. I was going to get my money's worth.

I bought a round of five and realized Shena was well gone. Her make-up was still fabulous. The last thing I remember is my sixteenth shot and Roo going home – she was bored and sober. I felt a bit queasy but like I had to look after Shena, who was getting clingy. That's not like her. Sometimes I can't help but feel she has emotions, and might even like me, but can't help not showing it in case her face slips off. In any case, we clung to each other. I thought of how we'd never had a chance to even kiss like we meant it.

As we draped ourselves round one another, Jude appeared somewhere to my right. I vaguely remember the gist of what we said. I cajoled him for not joining us in a beautiful tequila binge. He laughed a little, but wasn't amused. He looked sad, in fact. He was planning a big piss-up when he finished his exams. Shena thought he was boring, and said so, but offered him tequila and told him I was buying. He couldn't refuse enough. He asked me how was Belfast, and Roo, and all the usual. I remember his telling me his gran was ill. I can't recall why. I must have asked some question about his awful life, I suppose.

I was so over him!

He made his escape eventually, after what seemed a whole ten seconds. Not before I told him we would meet up the next day. Not before I told him I'd see him down the chippy, not before he agreed with an eyes-to-heaven smile. It was only a little smile, but not before time. Perhaps all the rest of what happened next was just to show him how I didn't care. I can't remember one more second after his turning and stumbling off.

When I woke the next morning I lay in bed for hours. It took me that long to think about leaving. I couldn't find my glasses. There was no one in the house, they were shopping I expect – not that the parents ever entered my mind. I realized somewhere how I was still pissed. Sixteen tequilas!

I met Roo on the way to the chippy. She sat me down at the roadside, I was so blind, she cackled away as I told her my sad tale of woe and amnesia. Not that it mattered, she knew the story. Mark had phoned full of glee in the morning. She led me, still laughing, til we got to the chippy and sat there to wait for Jude to show up.

'Twenty-one tequilas!' she laughed. 'You skinny wee runt!'

'Sixteen,' I insisted, but she knew better. She told me how she just had to see my face this morning. She couldn't believe I couldn't remember. She couldn't believe I was still alive. So in between snorts of risible derision (and a meagre smattering of almost-admiration) Roo told me my sorry story.

By the time I managed to sink the last round, myself and Shena were a tangle of tongues. We wept and we laughed and we propped each other up, reminiscing and planning a new life together, or whatever.

Our beautiful little dream was smashed to smithereens when Shena's horrified (and horrific) mates dragged her away. 'They thought you were trying to rape her, you big man!' Roo giggled.

'Entirely consensual,' I murmured. 'Probably.' Then I scraped a thought together. 'Or else she was raping me.'

I couldn't see a thing but Roo told me that we were getting funny looks. She disappeared for a while and left me gazing round the shiny, daze-inducing chippy. I tried not to drown in the glare of the oversized plastic posters. I could make out the mountainous processed food that loomed and glowed and gloated at us all. The images regurgitated themselves around the walls.

Roo came back stuffing chips in her gob.

'No sign of him?' munch, munch.

'I can't tell.'

'Well, there's no sign of him. Anyway! Where were you?'

'Shifting Shena. Horrifying friends.'

'So funny!' Gobble. 'Want one?'

'Bleurgh. No.'

'Anyway! Yeah!'

And so it continued, Carry On Tequila.

A mixed bunch of boys took me to the toilets, where I burbled about Shena.

'So would you go out with her? Again?'

'I could love Shena!'

'Aye, for a day,' Peter laughed.

'No!' I said, all concerned. 'I mean, a month or so.'

'Could be worth it,' Mark would shrug.

I didn't really want to know.

Jude propped me up in front of the bog. I managed to throw

up somewhere to the left, splattering my shiny contribution to the corners of the cubicle. I slumped in a sad little heap, it seems. When someone noticed how I didn't crawl out, Jude clambered across the top of the door and dragged me out for air. It was closing time. The bouncers were good enough not to kick my bones down their shitty steps. My comatose carcass littered the pavement. My glasses were smashed. It was, I gather, rather good fun.

Taxi-men refused to take me home. No one was brave enough to phone my parents, or theirs. As the idle guys whiled away their amusement, a passer-by decided to be my guardian angel.

'What's his name?' he shrieked. 'Oisín? Oshy? Can you hear me? Get this man an ambulance!'

Jude phoned his friends instead. Sad mate stole daddy's car, which was an adventure in itself, I expect. It seems they do it all the time. Jude is saving for a wreck of his own.

Anyway, they drove me home. They parked a bit down the road, and Jude carried me back to the house – the best minutes of my life, unconscious.

When they found the key in the pocket of my jeans, Jude carried me to bed – 'The room with me on the wall' – and tucked me in. That's when I woke fully dressed the next morning, and sat in the chippy with Roo. Waiting for him to come back and claim me.

JUDE

I met Oisín again. We were at the pub. Not together. He was dead friendly and everything. He always is. He was with that one Shena. I can't describe to you why she's the hatefullest meanest thing you'd ever see with the wee screwed up face on her. She was all over him. It was funny. She seemed to enjoy it anyway. I thought I should-n't be in the way. They were drinking tequila. He paid. He's nice that way. He doesn't mind. Maybe it's only if he wants something.

So they were really langered. He talked to me. He asked me would I do more photos – the ones were shit. So I said no cos once is enough. If it was no good well we tried. He got really hammered. Shit. He had near twenty tequila slammers Mark thingy said. You know. The ugly one. So he said again go on and I said as good as you were to me no and he looked like he'd swal-lowed the worm. He was trying to be raging. So them two shifted again. I doubt if they're back out but. And her friends made a show of them all. They pulled her away. He nearly fell over. He made it to the bog so he did. But not back out.

It was me that took him out. It made the night a good one. I
got over the door. The smell. Jesus. It was rotten. He'd puked in
the corner. It was funny as well. He was all slumped out of it. I
landed on his glasses jumping down but as long as he doesn't find
out. I'm bad enough.

Outside there was a whole big thing. They thought he was
dead. I had to phone John for his dad's car. He hates Oisín. Fair
play. He did it anyway. There was no puke or nothing. He was
empty. It was all right. Then his house was quiet. Good job. I
carried him up to bed. He's no weight at all. He reminded me of
this bird I found. I love animals.

I was walking up the road the other day when I seen this poor
wee bird on the footpath lying on its side and only moving one
poor wee wing. It was one of them brown ones. I knelt down like
Mother Theresa might have except she's dead. I stroked the bird's
poor wee head and he fluttered a bit. Then I cupped him up in
one hand. He clutched onto my fingers with these deadly claws
like you wouldn't believe. He hardly weighed a thing but just sat
there not looking at me. I thought he might shit all over my
hand or something. But I carried him all the way home anyway
looking to see if he was injured. It looked like half his tail had
been ripped off and one wing was scarred looking. He seemed
really dazed because he never moved. Not even when I tried to
fluster him up.

I took him round the back yard of an empty house where
there were loads of birds singing and squawking and everything.
He perked up a bit. I could feel him breathing now pulsing away

but not making any effort to fly. Then after we were sitting there for a while the helicopters came. Our native wildlife they are. He got all scared and flew out of my hand and tried to make it over the wall. But it was pathetic. He managed about a foot off the ground and scrabbled like a mouse I saw in my bedroom once. Then he hid his head in a corner.

I thought he might be hungry as well as scared so I went looking for worms in my Gran's back garden. But she said don't be stupid and gave me some breadcrumbs like the good sensible woman she is. Now these two wee brothers were in the house and you know how it is. The older one is dumb and ugly and stupid and the younger one is clever and cute and I told them and my brother who were all watching football about the Poor Wee Bird and I thought their little hearts would melt. Then the younger brother said he was Gonna Step On It And Squash It and I went back a disillusioned older man. Well I said how I was Gonna Squash the wee lad first. But the bird didn't eat any of the crumbs. Just kept flying scribbledy into different corners even when I dropped the crumbs on its ungrateful wee head and everything.

So I sat waiting for the miracle of flight to happen. But maybe it was because the helicopters were still around but the bird didn't fly. I got bored waiting so I threw a peg at it. It didn't notice or didn't care. The last I seen it was hiding away under the oil tank. So I said fuck it and it's probably dead now the poor wee bastard. I mean I'm still going to wash spiders down the plug and use traps to squash the mouses' skulls and eat chicken and everything. But it was just nice. Right?

So anyway Oisín wanted me to meet him at the chippy. He said so last night before he went splat. I would probably have went for the laugh but Gran has taken a turn for the worse. I've cycled up the last few weeks to read her prayers. She can't anymore. She has her relic and her beads and I don't get away with no holy water. She's happy enough.

I was wondering. Maybe Ciarán would want to go for a walk or something. Just to clear the head. Anyway. I reckon he'd want to know about Oisín and Shena. I seen the way he looks at her when she goes past in her red boots.

So I hope her and Oisín aren't together then.

OISÍN

I didn't even want to go but Liam rang and Roo begged me to come – 'We need someone else to pay for the taxi!'. Mum actually answered the phone to Liam at first. She said his name like as if it smelled bad ('I thought he was the weird one') and he sounded even more thick through technology. It showed up his speech impediments. So the idea was Neil was supposed to collect me once he'd managed to reassemble his car, and that stopped me short. My initial reaction was *anyone but Neil.* It would be weird because he and Seán used to be friends. I remember Neil coming round in his car when they had business to attend to. Then I thought, why not? It would be interesting to see if he had changed. So I said, I'll go if Shena goes, so I rang off to phone Shena.

Through all the giggles, her wee sister managed to tell me that Shena was off collecting German and French students for their half of the exchange-bargain, so there I was, stuck. She was supposed to phone me when (if) she was back at all soon.

So Roo phoned me again (obviously desperate), 'No but I really do want you here. All the girls are in Belfast' – and I said I wouldn't bother, Shena was away flirting with foreigners who might legitimately share her bedroom – and Roo said, 'OK, well Neil's collecting you at twenty to nine at the Bank of Ireland.' When I scraped my brain off the ceiling she told me just be there, love you, bye, gotta go, probably Liam being horny and her being pissed ('and what's new?' the cynics chorus).

So then I phoned Peter to tell him the horrible story so far (little-did-I-know) and hoped I would talk long enough to miss my lift, which I would have except Neil was half an hour late. I had to sit once I forced myself to get money from the slot bank machine thing, watching all the young trendies squawk about in their TopShop gear (not that I looked very different, probably pseudo-TopShop). So I was sitting there being late and someone had left 10p credit in the phone box and the receiver dangling in desolation (might have been God or just another pissed four-teen-year-old being dumped or something) so I phoned Roo, and Liam said 'No dude, he's coming' – he actually said dude, twice – I just sat around trying to remember what the fuck Neil looked like. What sort of a car?

So he looked like the sort of person you recognize when you see him but don't remember his face particularly, car was a wreck, I just felt awkward because I had bad memories of the guy, did-n't want his lift, didn't want to be there.

We had to buy the carry-out then, I have a half bottle of

whiskey left in the house but Mum was watching out, and even called out of the top window, 'Where are you going? Who's giving you the lift?', so I told her to piss off and skipped merrily on – anyway, the drive to Roo's should have been a lot more strained than it was – he asked after my dad, steered clear of politics and once it was established that neither of us were going to mention Seán, the journey glided by like a sigh of relief. We even agreed on some drinks we both liked, and some jocks we both hated. The funniest thing was the first girl I'd ever been with drove past in her own car, as lost-looking as ever. I doubt she recognized me. But people we knew – like the impassive giant footballing guy – stared at me, trying to work out what I was doing with this bad boy in his car.

So by the time we get to Roo's we're all buddy-bloody-buddy and Roo's on the phone to Shena, and totally pissed with it, waving a bottle of red in one hand (practically emptied) and the phone in the other. 'Talk to Shena!' so I did, all flirty, her being mock-moany but real-moany underneath it all, 'Oshy, you don't love me anymore!' 'Like I ever did!' because you can't humour her, she'll just dig herself deeper into your brain/dick/whatever organ you're currently thinking with. So she did come around, for a minute, just as I was cracking open my cognac, because who wants to get all fat on beer? Shena laughs when she sees me with a pint anyway, like it's too big and would consume me in half a swig (kind of like her, in fact). So when we're not alone, she doesn't pay me half as much attention, but we all follow Roo upstairs. It was a case of 'hello to Roo and her fulsome bosoms', barely encased in her leather bodice which Liam had great fun ravishing upstairs. They like to do their mock-gothic neck-scraping, stomach-clenching snog act, but really mean it, sadly, with death-metal bullshit refracting off the walls.

So all too soon Shena is flicking through Roo's clothes and denouncing everything in sight, but not before I manage to truly shock her.

It all started with Neil latching onto her, as he would with anyone, being Mr Smoothie, laughing at her jokes (not that she makes jokes, she just treated him with contempt and he had to pretend like they were jokes), but then I got talking to her because I don't think she liked the other guys very much (but probably appreciated their appreciation of her tits).

She was wearing white hipsters like only Shena can, being CK skinny, with a stripy blue and green halter-neck top – and her infamous green eyeliner. It should have all looked pretty awful, especially with the red-dye hair, but she has enough cheek to brighten me up anytime. She may not have been technically gorgeous but she acted it enough to make anyone believe it. Girls would be more difficult to convince ('The length of her nose! Too skinny!') but fuck it, jealousy screams.

So for some reason I said, 'You're brother is such a fag!' Of course the others immediately jump in with their odes to irony – 'The pot calling the kettle pink!' Neil guffawed, a little too enthusiastically, I remember – and Liam managed to fumble an almost coherent sentence – 'You – you said – he's – a fag! You're a fag! Faggiest fag!' and Roo just hadn't a clue what was happening, I think. The room was a boxy little mess, now that I noticed, but I was glad to see the graffiti and painting that I did for her birthday were still there. Anyway, Shena turned her newly blank face to mine and said 'So you're gay, Oisín?' but in a really natural way, her voice didn't squeak or anything, it was just that pale look. I think she looked frightened. 'Except for you, yeah,' I told her, and off she went to examine the jumbly piles of Roo's clothes. Most were black heaps and flouncy stuff in cupboards – 'I have no nice tops, I admit', but then Shena would suit anything – and she ended up borrowing a shiny silver skirt. When she went to the bathroom to try it on, Roo was like, 'I warned Liam not to tell Shena you were gay,' and she said it loud enough for Shena to hear it through the walls, but like I told her, 'Too late.' Not that I really gave a shit, cognac was my friend. I was waiting for it to kick my head in, which it didn't. It was only a quarter bottle, and there's me trying to catch up with these two who've been pissed since yesterday, when her parents left. Roo cheerfully told me that her parents were, no doubt, slumped in an alcohol-induced coma now anyway.

So in the bathroom, Shena was trying the skirt in various poses, so us wee girls went to do the gasp-it's-lovely routine and Roo, with rare tact, left it to let Shena change back again. So there was Shena in her 'mermaid dress' as Roo dubbed it, me, not waving but drowning – 'You don't want me to leave just as you're changing?' I said, and she just pounced (verbally speaking, I mean; can you say verbally speaking?): 'So close the door then.' Fuck knows what she meant, I just went 'Oh yeah, from the outside', so we laughed, and I felt freezing and awkward and began to feel that bit disorientated when I shut the bathroom door and turned to the too-blue room where it seemed nothing was changing, not even the CD. I tried switching the light on to lose the party atmosphere, but no one approved. Neil was even blocking real light with his by-the-window pose. Roo and Liam were still grappling. I was the only one in trainers and blue jeans, not drinking beer, not that I gave a fuck then or now, but there's something significant there anyway.

Shena made a point of borrowing Roo's skirt and I made a point of walking Shena home, just around the corner in this 'new neighbourhood' that her mother so approved of, a 'better breed of people', allegedly. Doesn't stop the visitors, I suppose. I was surprised at how glad I was to leave the house and be with Shena. She's never boring, she didn't even scrape up a 'So you're gay?', who knows if she even believed it? So we stood outside her house, which is pretty much pink and glowing with a shiny new bubble of a car, and we prolonged goodbyes, standing talking about nothing, jumping on each next non-phrase and pummelling conversation to death.

When we finally had edged our ways apart, round the car, round the fence, Shena making it to the house and flicking a goodbye over her shoulder as carelessly as flicking her hair – Davey came bounding over the grass shouting something like 'Oshy! The pecs on you, boy!' Because, presumably, I'm a skinny wee runt in a tight T-shirt. So now you know why he's such a fag – then he starts blabbering, as he does, and that sort of blabbering makes me have to stand back and get analytical, just to cope with all the words being thrown at me, and his beautiful face (Shena's, but refined and polished and glowing) and his über-straight stance. We were in later-Blur country, he's pointing through blinds going 'Look at the arse on that!' and telling me how the woman across the road from them is married to an alcoholic lawyer and he wants her to teach him to make love.

'Do you need someone to teach you to make love, Davey?', all unblinking eye-contact and ultra-soothing shrink-voice, and he's like 'Yeah', and suddenly embarrassed because he knows I'm going to offer so he changes the subject (sort of) by telling me how horny the exchange girls make him. I tell him 'German girls equa hairy armpits' and he says great and means it, enthusiasm makes him stammer and his cocktail of accents slips a gear, the Crossmaglen drawl sliding into place. He leaps over the fence to talk to some other bloke who gave him the fingers a minute ago, saying 'Stay there' like I'm his pet dog. But how sad is hanging round waiting for a neighbourly tête-à-tête to fizzle out? So I wave goodbye to all concerned, or unconcerned, Shena is nicey-nice and we've-got-to-meet-up-properly, but the exchange students are underfoot and silent, which somehow makes it all the more urgent for them to go, so I leave them to it. What am I running from? But that's just a stupid pissed question, so go back to the general squabble-friendly piss house and me and Roo do each other's make-up. Not before she takes a piss and replaces her tampon, dear me, no. She seems genuinely upset about Liam's inability/distaste for having 'a dump in front of me!' as if it's nor-

mal code of practice for all long-term (I say this loosely) rela-
tionships. Why anyone would find Liam's shit a beauty to behold
is beyond me, so I hurriedly restore a sense of glamour to the
bathroom ensemble with Roo's very limited make-up supply.

It's the only sub-artistic endeavour I've made in days and this
should depress me, but it's such fun, and I've nearly finished my
yukky but bland enough quarter bottle. It's enough to put a
sheen on even basic bathrooms and stubby eyeliner.

So Roo has this horrible chalky red lipstick on so it's the first
to go cos it's cheap'n'nasty, and she should emphasize her eyes cos
her lips are the fullish, naturally pouty sort and pretty wine-
soaked anyway. So she blinks and bats and gets rid of a lot of
under-eye make-up I've smudged on, because she reckons it
deadens her eyes, which is, of course, the whole point. She
brushes my face to make it paler, and does the whole eyeshadow
bit in a silver, the only colour she has, which is fair enough.
Because I like the necrophile style so much, I streak it on under
my eyes to intensify them, so I'm all starey. I look like a dead fish
instead of a zombie. It won't last long but it's all in fun.

Liam is mesmerized by bloke-in-make-up. Anyone else and
he'd be threatening to de-bone them like he does at the meat factory. Roo makes sure he's hustled off before he gets too boring –
'You're never interested in my make-up!' – by telling him, no,
really, fuck off, no, REALLY, Liam, get! Get out! Stupid bastard!
I hate you forever go away! Neil's on his own! – Neil's probably
sniffing her panties at this stage.

So the taxi ride is a giggle because Roo tries to set me up with the driver and I begin to feel a bit more in synch, and Dundalk is as shitty as ever so we all shine more brightly. Some scummy bar where the music is loud and the seats are wooden and uncomfortable and Roo takes over the jukebox. Liam becomes very concerned with the whole gay thing.

'So, like, why?' and I'm like, who cares? You can't help who you fall in love with, bla bla bla, and he's like don't say you're bisexual, fucking cop-out, and I'm shrugging and catching the eye of some beardy bloke who looks hard. Then he's telling me about losing his virginity at fourteen, and how 'I thought a girl's fanny was here', punching me somewhere in the stomach, 'but it was there', punching me in the balls. And then he's all surprised – 'You've never fucked a girl?' – and it's not like he feels sorry for me, he's just amazed. I'm a bit busy checking my make-up in the conveniently mirrored walls, but he's still a bit interesting all the same – so he starts to fret over how difficult it must be to be gay and when he's asking me how far I've ever gone I'm saved by Roo who wants someone to help her with the jukebox and manages to fight for about thirty seconds with Liam because he has no change or something. So Neil is passing round cigarettes which isn't like him but no one's complaining and I don't want one but have to hold Roo's when I'm telling her which buttons to press on the jukebox, so I try it anyway, but apparently I'm crap because it won't stay in my throat but comes out my eyeballs or feels like that anyway, my head's steamed up and I hate it. But I'd like to kiss Shena now to see if my smoky breath would make her lungs collapse.

It's weird but even now I can't remember who else is there or why things go so fast and I think we're all vaguely enjoying things but there's no reason why we should. Neil is telling me how he'd fuck the barmaid just because he could, and I think she's rotten in a normal, just ugly way and he doesn't care. 'Well you're gay,' he snorts, and I'm getting bored with being the token gay one, we're not a TV series yet.

Liam knocks off my glasses and I drain whatever's left in his pint when he's scrabbling for them on the floor and he wants to kill me for a bit til I promise I'll buy him two more and then he laughs and it's all OK and I can't remember a single other thing except stupid stuff like how the sawdust on the floor was fine enough to be sand and I remember walking on the beach once with Shena.

It was in Rostrevor, and we'd skipped out of some shit party because the raver and wobbly factions had begun to get on, the fights never happened, it was all very friendly and consequently dull. It was dusky, a mawkish haze drowned out the details of the ugly '60s houses, it was like being the only people left alive. Dotted buildings and plants and the sky going up forever made the place seem huge and insubstantial, we could hear the tide licking up the shore and only our footsteps had any solidity.

There were even these boats that had been left to rot in someone's overgrown garden, not silly wee boats, a couple of proper pirates. They were falling apart and I couldn't believe it. One was like a ghost, as big as the house that seemed so insignificant beside it, despite having people inside it – not that you'd notice.

The boat was shot through with weeds, and peeling, but it still looked capable of crawling away to die with dignity somewhere else. Shena thought it was funny.

She walked ahead of me, not taking anything in, just going to the beach. She slipped off her shoes when she got past the first crop of stones, and I sat on the ledgey bit that led to the water, watching her walk in the sinking sand. There was litter everywhere along this edge of the beach. All the usual, beer cans and crisp bags and cardboard and a shoe, and other things like a broken radio and even half a fold-up bed, substantial shit, in a little landslide that trickled through the grass and stones into the sand.

The funny thing was you couldn't tell if it had been left to fall into the beach or if it had been washed up from the sea – at least you knew, logically, what had happened – but you could imagine the other and it was sort of romantic. Shena had stopped and sprawled on a flat, smooth stone that's probably still there now. I could just see her poking at an inert crab with her bare foot. The soft kiss of the dying light made everything more beautiful and elusive all at once.

I got up from my seat in the rubbish heap and crossed the sand towards her, feeling so real by just treading into the scene, scarring shadows through the sand. Then all the water turned to beer and the sawdust reappeared and I put down my somehow empty glass and followed everybody else outside.

Liam lay on the ground by some fast-food place and moaned. Roo moaned about him moaning and Neil bounded off to get a taxi because he was the only sober one and where had he been all night? So Roo stomped off in her knee-high boots and a fetching scowl, and I sat down to listen to Liam and make sure he didn't choke on his tongue or anything. He felt shit, predictably, and even shittier about having to disembowel some frozen cow carcasses the next morning at seven. So I told him how this was less than five hours away and he was mortified and Roo came back with a drippy, sloppy burger that she managed to devour in about half a row's time, despite Liam telling her all the niggly bits of cows it was made from. He called her a cannibal and we had to carry him into the taxi.

Dundalk is a dullard town where the air is stale and rain never escapes the paving slabs. Desperate glimpses of neon expose the newest building façades as the tackiest of plastic, while older businesses have long since slipped into slumber. Their stone corrodes like the dreams of the old, only fragmentary memories give testimony to their stagnant ambitions. The moss that glisters prettily between cracks in the building blocks creates, by contrast, the impression of a thriving private ecosystem.

High-heeled chicks teeter among rails of cut-price finery til, purchases complete, they wander dazed into the street. Trimmed and grim young men contrive to look hard on high-street corners, their ballsy bluster obscuring a glance at romance and another drunk Friday, as spent as the wet and weaker shots of flying fists.

We arrived home to the sound of silence whispering its way through the empty estate. Roo's house looked like a big pink cake, waiting for us to devour it whole. The mood celebratory, we cracked the back door open and turned on the TV, the radio, something something something – yeah, I can't remember everything, we were happily pissed and bound to do something stupid.

Neil and Roo were trying out her keyboard, babbling about bands, singing very badly. In Roo's bed, Liam lounged in his underwear, scratched his unhairy armpits and mumbled about how I was OK for a fag. I propped myself up on my elbows, forgetting how dirty other people's beds are. As we talked about nothing much, our speech more woolly than the blankets, Liam lowered the bedspreads gradually, as if I didn't notice. He wanted to know how far I'd ever gone. I wasn't in the mood to discuss miserable exploits, I just teased him and he laughed and wondered out loud if I went in for casual cruelty. That wasn't his phrase, he was talking about blow-jobs. I was thinking of him cheating on Roo. I was thinking of me and him cheating on Roo.

'Would you?'

'What?'

'Give someone a blow-job and leave it at that?' and then Neil and Roo burst in. So we left it at that. Except that I had the great pleasure of whipping the covers off Liam's cold white body to parade his nakedness to the world.

Us three, anyway. We were the world. We were so happy and dumb.

Next thing I remember is being in the spare room, stripping for bed, leaving all my clothes strewn across the carpet, and rolling over in my snug single under the window that shone silver on my pillow. I was dozy enough to want to sleep, to drift, to feel the world go fuzzy – I was dozy enough to let Neil roll in beside me, and not wonder what the fuck was he up to? OK, friendly guy, I remember thinking.

'Wha's wrong wi' your bed?'

'Nothing, nothing.'

'What are you doin'?'

'Move over.'

So I do, and close my eyes to sleep away my stupidity. But Neil wants to talk. Neil has bedtime stories to whisper in my ear. Neil's fingers trace a repetitive circular pattern on my shoulders and his words are loud and calm and deep. His favourite story seems to be his one-night stand in a youth hostel with some English bloke. They didn't fuck. They weren't prepared. At this stage, I don't really care. I murmur back, 'But you're straight', and he says yeah. And I say, 'No you're not', and he goes yeah, I am. And I say how it's shitty to pretend, why do people pretend? If you fancy blokes you should say so, why can't people tell the truth? And he has a little sigh ready, and says he guesses he's not strong enough.

I lie there hating him and he stares at the ceiling, settles more comfortably into my bed. His naked legs crackle against mine, he says, 'Listen to them two up there'. The springs are springing away overhead, Neil is restless but appreciates the need to take his time. Pause.

Springy-springy-springy –

'So are you up for it?'

'No.'

'Why not?'

'I don't respect you,' and he doesn't move. His hand lowers the covers from our bodies, just a little. I absently note his toned chest.

'You haven't got a hard-on?' He's incredulous.

'I don't fancy y-shit. I feel sick.'

A familiar shot of acid rises through my gullet and sticks in my throat. My ulcer is leaking and trying to corrode me from the inside out.

'Do you need anything?'

'I need – it's OK. Let me out.'

Neil gets out of bed and I stumble across the mess we made, to the kitchen, everything buzzing and crackling like a telly on the blink, interiors cracking up, monochrome in moonlight. But I know Roo has a stash of tablets, she's a chronic alcoholic and understands these things. I rob her private pharmaceutical supply and let the tap gush enough for a mouthful – the hot tap, give a fuck – and in my head I'm crawling back to the bedroom, crashing into the door frame. Neil has settled into his own bed, broad shoulders propping up the wall. I stand with a hand to my hair, confused by the brightness of the uncovered window, the breeze that hushes gently through the room.

'I thought you might want some air.'

'I'll be good.' I'm unfazed by hanging out nude. Guess I'm not so insecure about some things.

'Come here,' he said, and I walked not too crookedly to the head of his bed, sat in the crook of his arm while he told me it would be all right. I hiccuped back at him, reassured, ill, apologetic for the bile that had killed the stillness of our thoughts. We quietly began to kiss and his arm folded round me. I kept thinking *this is wrong*. I thought of Jude, of how strong he would be. And I couldn't stop hiccuping.

Neil's dick was funny, like a scoop or something, but who's complaining? His hand clutched at my cock – slurp – and I mouthed apologies for being so sick. He was no more listening, our fingers seeking purchase in each others' bodies. My mind, fucked up, swarming, exploding in a second. I'm not talking orgasm, I just collapsed.

When I woke the next day from a humble little slumber, I reached for my glasses and remembered what had happened. Then I realized there are bits I can't remember, like how it all ended, or why, or where. I was in my own bed again, tucked up soundly, no idea how. Neil was gone.

Good.

I was sore, which ceased to surprise me when I went to get dressed and saw all the bruises.

There is something beautiful about a fresh bruise. It can glow from lavender to honey, burnt at heart, tender, ripe, reminding you of life. A chorus of them, swimming in my skin, went quite deep enough. I didn't speculate.

Roo and Liam came bustling in, full of eager questions like wasn't I glad I came, hadn't they been fun, mustn't we do it again? In an unsubtle way I signalled Roo to get her man gone. With scarcely an eyebrow raised, she did as she was bid. I made the mistake of telling her everything. Roo is good but her mouth is huge. She didn't keep from gabbling all fucking morning, and asking questions – like I could remember the answers – and exclaiming 'What about his girlfriend?' when she could safely pretend that Liam wasn't listening.

Of course, he heard the whole thing later, or picked it up in bits. I was in a lousy way for the rest of the day.

I said to her specifically don't tell a soul, I meant it. I should have known better. Roo's friends are soulless.

I didn't want anyone to know for his sake, which you can call as dumb as you want and I don't care. I don't like him any better, that's not what I mean. I mean it's not my duty to out him to the world. I don't want to. I'm happy to let him bugger off back where he came from.

It was cool that he kind of brought Seán back to me for a while, even though it was accidental. It's probably why I got sick. I was puking to the sound of gunshot salutes from Seán's big day out.

SNAPSHOT

Jude's granny lay in bed like a burst balloon. Party over! She had muttered herself to death that afternoon.

It hadn't been sudden, or painful, or even, he sorely reflected, very surprising to watch this woman die. As she settled into the nest of the bed and tucked the lace around her shoulders, he saw her features click into place for the first time he could ever remember. She ceased to be Gran and assumed a face, a body, a personality that rose above the easy complacency of an ancient family tie. He saw each wrinkle networking a once beautiful face, fine bones that stood starkly against the sinking flesh as if the skull was rising to consume all semblance of unique humanity. He saw the dead woman inside come to claim her inheritance, found himself placing a cold red rosary between her fingers and they prayed together for the first and last time. The stupidest thing, his head insisted, was that it wasn't out of place, or a chore, but that he wanted to. So the innards wound down, the brain sparked its last and Gran closed her eyes with a peaceful smile.

Jude felt cheated.

That was it?

He wanted histrionics, and passion, and a need to smash mirrors, ornaments, bones. Instead, a tom-tom heartbeat pretending to be sad. When all the time in the room ran out, only a fragile sorrow lingered in the air.

It was his loss. He cared. But not enough, yet, to cry.

His mum ran around with a teapot in her hand, chanting 'Do you have enough tea? Would you like a cup of tea? At least the food's fresh.'

Old people mumbled their condolences then resumed the function of their automatic cataloguing system.

'Which one's he?'

'The grandson, the eldest.'

'Is he married yet?'

'Jaysus no, he's only sixteen.'

'Is he only sixteen?'

'He's only the sixteen years of age. Now he's a good lad, he used to read Janey her prayers.'

Digestive biscuits were thoughtfully sucked.

'Will he be a priest?'

Jude shook many wrinkled hands and vaguely charmed the crazy folk.

'What are you doing now, lad?'

'GCSEs.'

'Whassat?'

'GCSEs.'

'Whassat?'

'Exams.'

'Aw! Bright fella. Smart one, eh? Ha ha!'

The place was starting to smell of old clothes. A woman wailed across the corridor, wailed dolorously for the soul of her friend.

Gran's teddy bears and dolls were as she had left them, Jude was glad of that. One bear in a snazzy scarf hugged a statue of the Virgin Mary. Two identical dolls stood either side of this touching display, their glass eyes reflecting the light of holy candles. Gran had ordered two from the magazine so she could preserve the symmetry of her altar.

It glowed in the hall. At the centre, Jesus and his bleeding heart, lit with a red lamp for that queasy feeling. He was flanked by St Martin and Princess Diana, their identical smiles followed you round the room. On top of the lot, resplendent in a bed his mammy made, Daniel O'Donnell and his sleazy wink.

Mum was talking. Jude wished she wouldn't. As she made herself dizzy with inane pleasantries, Jude gently took her arm and led her to the kitchen. She babbled a bit about 'refreshments'.

'That teapot has been empty for the last half an hour,' he said.

Mum stared at the teapot in her hand, chose to ignore him, straightened up her blouse and went to put the kettle on. Again. She'd boiled it four times and forgotten she'd done it.

71

Jude's wee brother was taken home by neighbours. Jude went to the door and put on his smile, thanked them for coming and for dragging off the baby.

He wondered if either of them would show up. That's when he saw Ciarán.

The imp was at the wake, sitting slew-eyed amongst women, noting their slack sack skirts and solid ankles. He politely nibbled on a salad sandwich. His eyes were blue and restless. Jude caught them from across the swamp of well-turned woollens and best hats; their suited deference was admired for moments only, before conversations resumed and swallowed up the spaces the boys left behind.

They must have talked, but neither can remember what it might have been about. Their memories are flat, like the air that thins when the night turns black. Remember the backdrop of chatter, filling up time like musical notes dropped on paper. Remember the melted sky and metal monster barracks, caged in for its own good, crouched by the roadside. Remember how tart the mist tasted.

Spiky little nails twitch over matches and a skinny body shudders in smoke. A bright and hungry afterimage remains emblazoned on the mind. Jude wonders how black his insides are turning.

'Fag?'

'Y – no.'

Remember smoke insinuating from the tips of his fingers, as the corpse cooled in the spare room.

And so they walked. They went to the lawns behind Ciarán's house, where shelter was plenty, bark was damp and streams broke the regularity of dirt track. So many overlapping layers of lace and grass – an embroidery, interwoven with short stories and tall tales, traditions, lies and romance. Flowers flourish, drunk as the bees. Clouds skitter across the skies, beams as bright as daisies highlight desires. The countryside surrounds, a fertile land where fairies breed alongside cows, and farmers tip their hat to the sun. The sweet smell of bullshit.

Hunkering by a tree, they watch terrier. Ciarán grabs the dog and flings him wide, sees him scramble through the air, land with a splash, oblivious to fear. Jude reflects that if they weren't alone, Ciarán would dive in after him squealing.

Their clothes, sensible and drab fabrics for the unkind season, have licked up mud from the banks, picked up stains from their clumsy stroll, remain rubbed in the dirt as the boys huddle deeper into their protective layers, watching the stream pass them by. Ciarán settles and skips a pebble. They don't so much as dabble as terrier paddles, claws stones, whines, whimpers and eventually bounds off beyond a fence, into a field, leaving the shivering friends behind.

They discovered they had nothing to say, but said it anyway.

JUDE

I have this gay magazine under my bed. It's not porno or anything. It's just a magazine. I remember buying it in the shopping
centre. I thought I was going to be arrested or something. I stood
there flicking through these football magazines. But I kept having to look at *Attitude* with some fit guy on the cover. It made
my heart go faster just knowing it was there. I'm so sad.

So after I looked around and no one was there I grabbed it. I
took it straight to the counter with the ad on the back showing.
In case anyone came. Good. Because then Mum and Dad walked
in. They just smiled like they were normal. They were glad to
meet me accidentally. It was one of them times when everything
zooms up into your face.

I got all embarrassed as Mum and Dad stood there in their
nearly matching jumpers. 'Look at that!' Dad said. 'He's embarrassed. We're not cool enough for y'boy!' He slapped my shoulder in a manly way. Mum said they'd give me a lift home. They
went off in different directions.

I slipped the magazine onto the counter and couldn't smile back at the girl who was smiling to show she didn't mind if I was buying a fag mag. I think I was able to say thanks when she gave me the change. I was pure red. I didn't open the Eason's bag all the way home in the car. I said it was a footie mag. I ran upstairs to hide it when we got home. I had to read it sneakily later. It made me sweat I swear to God. The back pages were full of these sex lines. They looked real sad. I could imagine two wrinkly sixty-year-olds groaning at each other down the phone. It was nearly funny.

It was full of talk about cock and arse which wasn't like a new concept but I thought it was sort of disgusting. It made my dick hard but. I had a big mad wank over this black guy with short bleached hair and baggy combats. Fuck. I nearly cried. I was pumping so hard spunk hit me in the face. It's sort of funny cos blacks and faggots is where Gran wasn't so clever.

Gran's attitude to black people was 'they're alright as long as they stick to their own'. I asked why. She said 'Because they start mixing and then you get lots of little half-castes running round and who wants them?' So I said you're not allowed to say half-castes. She really made me angry. I said it's mixed race. Anyway. What about John Devlin? Sure he's mixed race. Sure he's black. Gran knew him cos he used to deliver her vegetables. Gran said 'John Devlin's no black man. He's a gentleman.'

I told Gran I was going to take home a black woman and she said 'Aye you would.' Then I told her I'd bring home a big black man and she started to mutter about 'gays and homosexuals'.

One other time we were watching telly together. It was me and Mum and Gran. Dad was off down the pub. That's not weird. We were watching a documentary about sex. This man we never saw got to follow people into nightclubs to watch them get off with someone. They did a token gay club.

When it came to the bit where men started rubbing each other's sweaty bodies I glanced at Mum. She nodded at the telly with a cartoon look of horror on her face. As if to say 'Get that off!' I said no and woke Gran up from her doze. She scratched her leg. She used to leave flakes of skin on the sofa. There are still some there between the cushions. She saw the two horny bastards tonguing each other and went into a fit. 'Jesus!' she shrieked 'I'm modern but I'm not that modern!'

I ordered a back issue of *Attitude* that never came. At least it probably did. But I never got it. It was supposed to have stuff on teenage prostitutes. It looked cool. Oisín would like it.

I remember finding Mum near in tears one morning. She must have found it. Amn't I smart? It must have been in clear plastic so I better avoid the postman too.

Maybe it was my fault for telling her I wanted my bedroom painted pink. I was only messing. 'Not many men like pink' she said. All serious. 'Your grandfather liked pink.' She said it like that made it all right.

Not long after I found a *Sacred Heart Messenger* under my pillow. I'm used to that sort of thing from Mum. She's superstitious. Her and Gran would always near drown me in holy water when I left the house.

What's so holy about it I wanted to know. Gran said it was blessed. I said it was priests' piss. 'I think your mother's right' Gran said 'You are confused.'

So the *Sacred Heart Messenger* magazine was normal for them. There was a picture of a kid with a mucky ice-cream face on the cover. It said he was a Problem Child. He was acting downright bold and in need of a good talking to. It made me mad cos it was so stupid. But then I got to the bit about homosexuality.

I hate the word homosexuality. It makes me think of someone wired up wrong. Like you're in a clinic and there's no cure. Like someone patting your head cos you can't help it.

The *Sacred Heart Messenger* told the story of a sensitive boy who went to the city and came back 'wearing pink T-shirts and suchlike'. This was all very disturbing and distasteful for his family. Luckily only 1 per cent of the adult population is affected which is rubbish. Homosexual feelings are not evil so long as a homosexual doesn't act on his unnatural impulses to wear pink T-shirts. Lesbians don't exist or something.

I was so angry I wanted to tell her all about Oisín. Except there was nothing to tell.

I threw the stupid paper at the wall. I went to the bathroom to splash my face with cold water. I saw my ugly reflection and realized I was old and spotty and all my features were slipping out of place and I put my fist through the mirror. It was a big thump. Silvery bits were crushed in my knuckles. Big pointy chunks fell into the sink. All this blood began to trickle. It splashed on the floor like little flowers.

'I'm not painting your room after that' was all Mum said.

I went for a walk with my dog last night. It was the full moon. We headed off at four but it was bright. He had great fun snapping at my ankles on the stairs. The town felt wider being empty. It was so calm. I couldn't lie still for longer than a minute.

First we went to the Mucky Lane. The dog liked all the shit and junk. It was more scary at night. All quiet. The trees were drier and twistier and scratchier like they were – anyway I walked to Ciarán's house. It was dark like all the rest. He says he doesn't dream. We looked up at the blinded windows. Didn't hear the machinery scream from the park behind where they're doing it up.

What I really wanted to do was throw stones up at Ciarán's window. Maybe just to hear a noise. There was no point but. He would be asleep like he was meant to.

I had the Lawns in my head. I was thinking of how the water would be louder than anyone realizes. It goes in a stream under the road where Shena's mother crashed into the wall once. You would always say Shena's mother. Not Shena's mum. She wears trousers and has roundy gold earrings. Usually. Very Eighties. It's funny. She always keeps her brightest smiles for my mum or whoever in their tracksuits.

I don't know when but I kept on going past all the hedges and lazy little midgets doing circles in the air. We lost each other at the Post Office. The dog went off to chase a dog. He went round by the corner where the houses are busted. Where the army threw yellow paint on the IRA slogans.

I felt itchy on my face cos I was getting new spots. I thought it might be healthy. The air felt cold and clean. I wasn't thinking about nothing but I knew I'd walk real far. I knew I'd walk much further than I told myself I would.

The missing dog was like a space at my feet. It was an excuse to go wherever was far enough. At the Lawns I turned at the bridge to watch the water. It was furious. The white broken splashes went angry and disappeared.

I didn't stay long. I looked at the lorries being dead in all the broken bottles. Weird bits of useless metal were in chunks all around. The houses were fresh because it started to get light and new. It was important to walk on. Not scratching my face.

I stopped for a piss past the Creggan houses. I like pissing outside. It was steamy and left the grass glittering.

On the road past Silverbridge them twisty corners nearly killed me. At the first one I realized the danger. A blind turn and a car might smash me. I started to run to round the corner quick. I wasn't turning back. I'd already done about four miles and seen what a new start did to the day. It washes it out to start again. It was like Oisín's watercolour of me standing on a broken rung in a fence. Facing the sun. My face is all screwed up. I look stupid. I don't mind.

But at the corner I heard hooves. A cow bawkying round the bend. It was clap-trapping along. More heavy than a car. It bolted. She looked me in the face and bellowed and buck-lepped. Was confused. Then the milk-truck came. Swerved til the cow scrambled the ditch tripping over all those knees. I stood gawping. The

JUDE

milkman went with a salute. I ran on forgetting the cow. It
jumped the wall into the road. It nearly hit me with its head.

I went steady then. Trying to ignore it. Not being sudden or
letting it get scared. She watched me. Wary. Slow. Probably
exhausted.

I told the story of the cow and the milkman in my head the
next bit of the road. It's the sort of thing Oisín would like. Milk-
men crashing cows by mistake. Not like. But enjoy. He'd laugh
at the bit if the cow killed the milkman. That's the way he is.

I knew I wouldn't stop til I got to Mullaghbawn. The sky was
pale and blue but the moon still hung around. It was like half-
ate Communion.

The milkman passed me again at the Aughanduff phone box.
He slowed down and asked, 'Are you going to Camlough?'
Maybe he was lonely. I said no but thanks. He waved and went
on never to be seen again. Not by me anyway.

It was just foot foot foot all the way. The chapel was too clean
to be real. The road was – I hardly remember. Cracked. The bus
shelter at Tierney's was all schoolkid graffiti. I stopped to read it.
All about the RA and Debbie is a slut. There's no phone. I wondered if Mum and Dad were going spare. I sort of expected him
to run me over any second.

There was a car in a ditch. About halfway to the bridge. I
clambered in to take a better look. Glass sprinkled in the grass.
The paint was newly scratched. There wasn't any bodies but the
blood was wet and fresh. I dipped my finger in. Then I realised
that was dumb. The seats were out of place. I don't know how. I

found a girl's licence lying in the field. It must have been thrown clear. I thought I'd post it back. But maybe she was dead? So I put it in my pocket and thought I'd wait to hear the news. They must have been drunk on the way home from Newry. I think I know her brother.

There was a bust football too. Further up the road. I kicked it through the rows of old folks' homes until I got bored. Which was soon.

I found a house by the bridge that was full of broken stuff. Wood. Plastic. Concrete dust everywhere.

I made the call through the operator. Maybe she listened in. Mum couldn't believe I walked to Mullaghbawn. 'You'll be lucky if he comes to pick you up' she said sensibly.

I had a look at the house where Ciarán used to live. I must have looked forever. You know. Three or four times. I was nearly surprised when he didn't come to the window. There were net curtains so I couldn't see in.

Dad picked me up. He was raging.

Gran's was the first wake I was at. It wasn't so bad as it might have been. Mike was saying it would be a terror and shaking hands. It was in her house. It was just big enough. We had her in the back bedroom. Hers was too crowded with stuff.

'It's nice' Mum said. 'Because she picked that wallpaper herself.' All the women nodded.

She looked the same. I stared too much. I expected her to

breathe. The only bit I found weird was how everyone talked so much about other stuff. The price of fields or the President on the telly. I felt like waving my arms about and going 'Hello? There's a dead woman lying in her coffin. She's my Gran. Stop ignoring her.'

Her fingers were very white. They looked too full. Her red rosary beads were wrapped very tightly through them. Entwined.

'It's a beautiful coffin' someone said. 'Isn't that blue frill unusual?'

'It's a feature' someone said.

I helped to pass round the sandwiches. It was awkward when someone tried to shake my hand. There were biscuits as well. I learned not to ask if they wanted tea. You have to push it in their face and raise your eyebrows. Then they won't refuse.

'Aw this is the grandson? Fine fella. Doing exams? Smart.' As if not everyone gets an equal chance to fail them.

There were plenty of people. The house was packed. I kept wondering if he was going to be there.

People who I never liked I had to feed. We all had to stop Mum going mad. Spilling tea or dropping things. We had so many kettles on the go we blew the fuse. Tripped the switch. Whatever.

Luckily the undertaker had candles. He was unobtrusive. He melted in with them. While an electrician got to work with a knife we lit up 'the remains' with holy candles. If anyone said 'the remains' I was going to kill them. She's my Gran. I mean she's still my Gran.

The house was very cold. 'Why are all the windows open?' I wanted to know. The curtains were spooky. They snapped or glided depending on how heavy they were. The ones in the spare room with Gran and all the whispery-chattery tea-sippers were net. There were spidery shadows.

'We have to keep the house cool' Dad said. 'Or else the body will sweat.' I suppose he meant decompose.

Dad was being very good. 'There used to be drink at these things' he said nearly fondly. He sort of smiled and took a big bite out of this crumbly cake that a busy woman had made. There were currants stuck in his teeth. Like flies on the grille of a bonnet of a car.

He's really sweet to the baby. He hoisted Patrick up on his shoulder when he was too tired to be cooed at. 'Gran's dead Patrick. Gone to Heaven.' I mean we tried explaining. 'She's broken. She's not working anymore' I said. But Mum said shut up.

Dad played with Paddy's toes. Everybody smiled. I collected the empty teacups and dropped a plate of biscuits by mistake. 'Not to worry' some woman said. 'You were just carrying too much.' As if I was going to burst into tears because of some crumby carpet.

Time went very slow. Even though we all had things to do time went very slow. It was better to have things to do to take our minds off 'Gran is dead'. Even though Gran being dead was why we all had things to do.

Oisín never came and I sort of didn't mind. Ciarán was there. But I never expected him and his parents. He looks like a delicate mix of them both. He belongs in a forest. Hiding under mushrooms.

We went outside for a bit. We both agreed together. It was all done on the quiet. I thought I should maybe feel guilty about not spending seconds weeping over Gran but so what. We weren't going to do anything. Not obscene like.

He had combats on. The green patchy sort. It was kind of funny. You know the army wears them but it's still OK. I mean Ciarán is a marginal RA-head I suppose. But wearing the uniform makes him tough. His hair is floppy and blond but. He had a plastic jacket on and didn't look stupid.

He took cigarettes out of a pocket at his knee. His lighter was green too. It matched his eyes but I couldn't see them. Not then. His face was heavy and hidden under his fringe. It made him look vulnerable. But he knew that.

I reckon Oisín did Sociology and Psychology and all that bullshit cos he was looking for answers. I mean there are no answers. I reckon most people want to try it. Not everyone. Just lots. It's just a question of how much and how scared they are of being found out. And how they get into the habit of marriage and not upsetting people. We just do what's expected of us – I mean I do too. All my science. Putting samples into glass and writing my unimportant totally predictable answers in a column and if it's wrong then I change it to what it's meant to be. I mean it works. I keep my head down and that's fine and hardly anyone bothers me. Or notices.

Sometimes I feel like a bit of me was killed. I can't tell people what I really think. I say what I have to. I sit in Pastoral fucking Care and hear my teacher tell us how we can't blame homosexuals. We should feel sorry for them. It's not their fault they're genetically kinky. And I think of all the people sitting in rows and I know – I mean I just know – how they feel it too. And we all sit in silence absorbing this with our faces on the floor.

He had the decency to cough. There was of course that chap in the year above us. Mentioning no names. Although it was obvious. Quite obvious. He dyed his hair. He 'came out' (teacher crooked his crooked fingers) during one of these discussions. In despair. In one way coming out was rather brave though naturally bisexuality was an ill-considered choice – however erm if anyone in the class thought he might be homosexual –

'Doubt it.'

'What?'

'Doubt it' I heard myself say. And looked up from my sweating fingers to find half the class staring at me and the other half still staring at the floor. Only more.

I think someone must have noticed the hopelessness in my voice. I thought it was kind of obvious.

Ciarán didn't talk about school. He hardly talked about anything. We just felt kind of right. We sat on the coalbunker til our arses were too cold. Then we decided we'd walk a bit.

He blew smoke out his nostrils. You could tell he loved himself. It didn't matter. We didn't go far.

Past the house slowly. The laces on his runners followed him like worms. He stopped to squeeze a foot in a gap in the gate. Swung a bit with his back to me. His hair gleamed like a girl's.

'Are you going to Anto's party?'

'When?'

'Next Friday. His parents are in Spain.'

'I dunno.'

Ciarán didn't say anything. The gate kept on creaking. His shadow stretched and shrank in synch.

'I'm probably supposed to not go out for a month.'

'Aw right. Yeah.'

'I might go anyway' I said. Then slid down on my hunkers to play with the weeds that grew up from under the stones.

Back in the house Dad was telling stories. Some people listened and laughed out loud. Others thought they should whisper. Or at least murmur and chat about unhappy things. No one minded that I'd slipped out for a while.

'You do what you feel like doing' Mike had said. Mike always says stuff like that. He's big into getting his own way. But not subtle.

The priest came to sort out readings. We all knew I'd be doing them all. So I picked the one about 'The Lord is my shepherd there is nothing I shall want.' Everyone knows that one so they don't have to think about it.

I wondered if Gran would be pleased with her 'send-off' as she called it the odd time. She didn't talk about dying. She didn't want to. Sometimes she'd say things like 'I don't want yon one at me send-off. She'd be wailing like a nanny-goat!'

I think I'm right to not believe in Heaven. But it's nice to do things properly too so I didn't mind readings.

Towards the end Gran got bored of praying. We sat in her

bedroom looking at the birds out the window. She couldn't get over how they didn't die by sitting on telephone wires.

'You know' she would say 'I'm awful bored.' There were times she could hardly talk. Sure she wasn't fit to be entertained. She would lie in the bed and barely wrinkle it. About as substantial as chalk dust. She would sigh at herself and how she had failed. She would worry. 'I've gone off prayer' she'd say. 'Everybody's bored' I would tell her. 'We're all bored. It's the modern age.'

'Do you think?' she'd say and stare at Our Lady on the wall. 'We didn't used to be –' then maybe she'd close her eyes for a few moments and concentrate on speaking correctly.

'I want' she'd say 'to get drunk.'

SNAPSHOT

The sun made him damp and his backpack weighed him down. He began to feel the black smudges loosen, turn to grease across his face, like some shadow melting amongst the traffic. He excused some cars to study the landscape.

The ditches were lined with his mates, lying on their bellies and occasionally shifting their rifles' point of view, the rifles that had to be lighter than they looked.

It was too hot, the fields alive with insecticide, the hedges humming, the drone of helicopters fading overhead; mechanical wasps on rotary leave. Headfucked women on their knees. Cut-knuckled, wounded, nitrogen blood. Joints of steel. The weather's good.

The busy haze was not what he'd expected of Northern Ireland – he had anticipated the dumb and shell-shocked buildings, burnt-out garages in dispirited estates, dead-eyed children whose folks had long since given up. He had not expected terrorism to be invisible. Sure, there was graffiti, sloppy slogans and half-arsed propaganda – but it was all too easy to imagine some schoolkid colouring in those rough-cut posters in between homework.

The signposts were the only visible heritage of violence – *If There Was No Political Violence There Would Be No Political Prisoners*; *Free All Prisoners of Conscience Now!*; *Oh Mull of Kintyre, The Bodies Wash into the Sea*; *IRA* (in tricolour); *Barrack Busters*; *My Brother Is Not a Criminal* (on a board behind a dozen white crosses).

Where was the passion? Where was the bloodlust and hatred and blind injustice? Instead, a little townland of cracked shops and crumbling edges, empty threats in bastard English.

Absentmindedly, he scuffed at the cheap tarmac that crumbled like biscuit under the heavy rubber sole of his regulation boot, shared his irritation with someone else, successfully completed the routine check of a lumbering cattle lorry. The driver said no more and no less than he had to by law, staring impassively ahead, implicitly hostile. He could have made it all more difficult, insisted on a search or busied someone up with the walkie-talkie, but why bother? It was the feeling of being up against amateurs that offended him most.

The last vague feeling of something unresolved slivered in his brain as a sniper's bullet spun through his chest, exploded in his heart, turned him inside out across the black and sweating roadside.

A couple of miles away, Neil also lay on his belly in a ditch. He dismantled his rifle and wondered how he should approach the next problem.

JUDE

On the night of the party I told Mum and Dad I was going round to Mike's house to do a project. That's why I had to take my schoolbag. They were teaching Paddy how to become a moron like everybody else. I don't know. Barney was dancing with his puppet kids maybe. Anyway. Dad said he'd give me a lift. I hoped the bottles of wine wouldn't clunk when I lugged them out to the car.

I nicked them from the fridge out the back. In the shed we have this old fridge full of wine. Dad only drinks spirits these days.

So anyway. We sat in the car and waited for it to get warm. Dad pretended to be interested. What was the project about? Had we started it yet? I would be trying to explain when he'd say something out of nowhere about the house McEntees were building. Or how such-and-such never came to the wake.

Dad is a mad bastard sometimes. Once at a football match the referee gave a goal to Killeavy. I mean it was a bad decision.

But Dad decked him. He broke three of your man's teeth and had to be restrained. Cross won the re-match.

I told him I'd stay over at Mike's. He said good cos he was heading to the pub. He said to watch my manners. I would have said the same but I was scared.

So Mike was nearly ready. He was on the phone to Fiona. His mother asked what was in the bag. She was being fussy. She gasped cos I'd got awful tall. You know. Stuff. So I said I brought an extra jumper cos I was cold. She just laughed. I mean she didn't believe me. But not in an embarrassing way.

I could hear *Winning Streak* on the TV. Some old guy was winning a fortune. Mike's mum said how she had to see Dinny win loads of money. She disappeared into the sitting-room saying 'I hope we're as lucky some day!' I never seen no more of them. I could hear the TV but.

The house was all bright. I put down the bag. I tried not to stare at the way the house is all wooden. Floors and walls and ceilings. It's like being in a box. The kitchen is huge. The washing machine was going without making a clunking noise.

Mike was yapping away. I stood there til he had finished. They had a mirror but I couldn't face it. I looked at the back of Mike's head. He didn't say hello or anything.

I felt a bit stupid.

'Bring it' Mike said. 'And one for Jude too.'

'What?' I said but he ignored me.

'I don't care' Mike said. 'No. Yes. I don't know. A guitar I suppose.'

So I didn't bother to wonder.

Mike had loads of hair gel on. He never has spots and looks like a waxwork.

'I have to go. This bollox is waiting for me' Mike said turning round to wink at me. I looked away. I couldn't be bothered.

'Whatever' he said and hung up. He thinks he's running all our social lives. He thinks we have social lives. You know. Not just live lives.

'Did you get a corkscrew?' he said.

'No.'

'Ah. Jude never gets a screw' he said. He checked his hair in the mirror before he led me upstairs. 'We'll be going now. I've to change the Nikes.'

We wandered round for a bit. We wondered where to drink. I thought the car park where Mike's mum dropped us off. We had to pretend we were going somewhere first.

We ended up looking at the fountain. All the light from the cinema and hotel and the stars lit it up.

'You could paint that' Mike said.

'No' I said.

'Why not? You're good.'

'It'd be hard.'

'But you're good.'

'But it'd be hard to get the way the light. Uh. Moves' I said.

'Is she gone yet?'

'Huh?'

'Huh?' Mike said sarcastically. And looked around. 'Me ma.'

'Oh. Right.'

'She's gone. Come on.'

I followed him into the corner where the shadows meant no one like the army or no one could see us.

'No but you could paint that. I've seen the way you do detail.'

I didn't say anything.

'You're fucking useless' Mike said. And let out a big sigh. 'You won't even say you're good when you know you are' which made me smile. But he couldn't see.

Mike took charge of the bottles. I'm too clumsy. He did it well. But then I knocked over the first bottle. It smashed. The wine gurgled out in a puddle. I made a grab for what was left.

'It's just the top smashed' Mike said. I tried to hold the bottle up to the light.

'Is it OK to drink it?' I said.

'Sure.'

I wasn't sure.

'What about the little bits?'

'It's a clean break' Mike said. 'The little bits'd be washed out anyway.'

'There's about half left' I said. Encouraged.

'That's all you'll need' he said. So I told him to fuck off as he screwed away and laughed at me sitting there with half a smashed bottle of wine.

We were crouched first but then sat in the gravel. I looked for bits of glass til Mike took the bottle off me and poured a bit into his mouth.

'It's alright' he said.

'But what if?' I said.

'Nothing' he said. 'What's a wee tiny bit of glass going to do? It'll go right through you.'

So I took a drink. The edge was a bit jagged so I was careful about my lips and tongue.

'It'll only stick in your neck and choke you.'

I gurgled. Like the broken bottle.

'Or enter your bloodstream and pierce your heart.'

'Bastard' I said. But I drank it anyway.

The sound of the town was of some alco singing and a stupid alarm that rang forever. The cold made my muscles tense. So did Mike sitting beside me. His elbow brushing me. By mistake I suppose. And the way he'd talk about the women he'd ride.

'Shena has the best set of tits on her!' he'd say enthusiastically.

'She's a bitch.' More wine.

And he'd sing 'Hey Jude' to piss me off. And he drank yon drink quicker than me. I was swilling every mouthful round to find glass. And he'd keep going on about the fucking fountain. I sat for ages thinking about nothing. But listening to him rant on.

'Shena wants me.'

'Hmmm.'

'Fuck you! She does.'

So I watched a helicopter swing out of sight. And he said nothing but swigged. So I said 'How do you know?'

'She wants me. She's all fucking over me.' He put his arm around my shoulders and leant in close. I felt his stubble brush my ear and his winey old breath in my face. He huddled up and the car park turned multicoloured. He started to speak but I didn't hear all the words. I was trying to control the tugging in my keks.

'She's always like – Come and play with me Mike. And does this big eyes thing.'

So I tried to laugh.

'Glass splinters choking you up Jude?'

He had his bottle in the hand that hung at my shoulder. He pointed it at the fountain. I tried to shrink into his armpit. On the quiet.

'You'll choke on all that glass' he said. Louder than he should have. 'And it'll all come out in a big shower. And you'll be lying dying. And it'll be like yon fountain – all glittery – and depressing.'

Now Mike talks a lot of shite when he's drunk but yeah. The fountain's depressing. It was meant to be all celebratory but fell like it was crying. And weak.

I didn't care. I wasn't listening. I liked the buzz of his breathing in my ribs.

'You could paint it in specks. It'd be good in speckles wouldn't it?'

'Weird' I muttered. I didn't want to spoil things but I was pissed off with this fountain.

'And shimmery. And splashes. Little splashes.' Swig. Shut up.

'I do normal art' I said.

Mike didn't say anything. He sort of woke up. And collected himself. He tautened and scratched his ear. He nearly took his arm off my back.

'Oisín Grant could do it.' I couldn't help myself saying that. The way the water splashed reminded me of the time my class was making models in the art room. Oisín was there cos he was doing his A-Level Art. He was always there this period extra. Happened to be the same time I was there.

Anyway. The models were papier-mâché. Mine was crap. I was doing fiddly bits. Like fingers. It wasn't very big about the size of a cat. But fiddly.

So he was washing a brush and watching us. Me. So he said 'Need a hand?' And I sort of said 'OK' without looking at him. Cos maybe all the rest of the class were smirking. And we both went on dipping our hands in watery glue. And getting sticky. And building up the wee stupid kid with bits of scrap paper. The glue dripped everywhere. Spunky. It was fun.

'Oisín' Mike said and spat. He took his arm away and drained his bottle. 'Faggot' he said. He stood up. 'Are you right?' he said. And shook his legs out. 'Fucking cold. Come on.' He kicked me out of whatever dwam I was in.

'That's us' he said.

I tried to be enthusiastic but I liked sitting there being miserable for nothing. I chucked the broken bottle at some crap car. It smashed against the wing mirror.

Mike laughed. 'You're mental' he said.

It was an inappropriate response. I tried to laugh back. And stumbled up as Mike strode over to the car. I rubbed my knees cos they were sore. Mike got his cock out to piss on the car that I just threw the bottle at and smashed.

I mean it's not like I never talked to him. Oisín. I mean I even thanked him. That time. 'Thanks for the help' I said when we put all the scraps away. And left our kid sitting on the shelf.

'All art is a cry for help' Oisín said. And slung his cloth bag over his shoulder. And walked away.

I fucking hate when he does stuff like that. Weirdo.

We met up with the rest like we were meant to. Outside the Offie we all needed more. Mike began to mix. I watched. Shena talked to me. Not him but. He was trying to impress Paul with his own interpretation of last Saturday's match. He was stone useless but wouldn't say. It was all Conor's fault. Cos Conor wasn't there.

Anyway. Me and Shena looked at them. And looked at the ads in the Offie window. And shrugged. And went in.

I mean I still didn't like her or anything. But at least she'd talk to you. I think she might be jealous of me and Oisín. Not that she should be. But. You know. She notices things.

She took a selection of Bacardi Breezers out of the fridge. The dopey looking guy rang them through the till and then asked 'Have you any ID?' I concentrated very closely on the different prices of draught-flow and crappy Guinness. And looked sideways when I heard him laugh. She showed him her bus-pass. And a big smile.

97

'Hurry up you' she said to me. I was scared of dropping the tins everywhere. 'He's a bit slow. You have to be nice to him' she told the man. Who looked pure stupid. Which made me feel a bit stupider really.

I hovered between conversations on the walk to Anto's house. I found a quiet corner in his brother's bedroom. The house was a bit mad. It was packed. There were strangers.

'There are millions of people I don't know' said some silly cow in a jester's hat.

'Sign of a good party' some twat told her. His hair was ginger but he dyed the fringe purple. I know him from hurling. He thinks it's clever to poke your ankles with the stick and always dives. He sickens my happiness.

I was getting morbid wondering what terrier was doing. Last time I seen him he was playing with a dead rat in the field behind Ciarán's house. And where was Ciarán?

Anto came over. He just got his head shaved.

'Jude boy! Good to see you!' So I grinned for his trouble. 'Are you alright?'

'Yeah.'

'You look a bit peaky.' His eyebrows are crazy. They're fatter than his moustache. His moustache looks like a caterpillar died on his lip. Oisín said that once.

He sat down for a second. And asked me who I'd seen. I said I'd seen no one good. It was loud. There were three CDs playing.

I could hear them all. My head was wrecked. I didn't want to talk to no one. I was sick of people's heads and their hellos and their how are yous and dumb boyfriends rowing with their fucked-up girlfriends and the one who can't find the bloke who she was meant to shift and some cunt who ruined his shirt and picked a fight with any wanker who was shorter and uglier than him and that fucking Anto and then I realized I was saying all this out loud cos Anto's eyebrows started sniffing each other.

'Aye mate' Anto said. 'You're well gone.'

So we clinked cans. He clinked cans. I just opened another as he stumbled off grabbing Lisa by the waist as he went out the door. She squealed. Ugly bitch.

I don't know how long I sat there being sorry for myself. It was at least three Oasis songs. Boring. Sleep.

'Jude!'

'Huh?'

It was Cathy. She sprang up and down. And leaned over. And squished her tits against me giving me a big hug. I give up trying to work out if she fancies me or not.

'Mike is shifting Shena!'

'Hum.'

'Oh my god! You don't fancy him do –'

'Shut up!'

I told Cathy one night we got stupid together. Whiskey. In a tiny bar in Carrick. She was planning to seduce me. It didn't work. She wondered why. Out loud. So I told her. Out loud as well. Not just. You know. Implied.

She had to go to the bog for a very long time. She came back composed but. And curious.

'So is it all up the bum?' was the first thing she said. I was like no. And she was like what then? And I was like shush. And she said who cares? And I said me. And all the blokes who'd kill me. And she laughed. And I said why was she laughing? And she said they were all scared shitless of me anyway. And would be more if they knew. She said I'm a moody bollox. Like I'd rape them to death. Yuk.

'No one can hear us!' Cathy screamed. Cathy always thinks no one can hear us. 'And they're all blootered and they'd forget! Lighten up sexy!'

I wish she'd stop.

'There are loads of cute men!' she went on. Settling down on a Man United cushion. And nicking one of my stinking Guinnesses.

'Man United!' she laughed. 'That could be you and Mike.'

'Fuck off. And shut up.'

'Oh! Fuck! Joke!'

'I don't fancy Mike' I whispered. There was no one else there but I whispered anyway.

'But yous went for a carry-out on your own' she said all sly. She pulled her knees up and across my chest. Her hair is very long and blonde. A strand of it sank into my Guinness.

'What did he say?' I said. Confused. And she burst out laughing.

'He said you never shut up as usual!'

'Very funny.'

'About Oisín Grant' she said. And took a sip of Guinness all casual. And wiggled her feet. Waiting for me to do something moody and bolloxy.

I was pure red. 'I didn't.'

'Shut up about Oisín?'

'Shut up.'

'Isn't that what I said?'

'Fuck off. You're boring.' Then I turned away and started to cry a bit into my shoulder.

She was all apologetic. She put her arms around me. It was nice. I made her stop but cos in case someone was looking. I might have spilled something. I didn't care. Anto's brother's room was shit anyway.

Cathy stroked my hair and we had a conversation. I'm lost for a good conversation. You know how rooms smell weird in other people's houses? Well we sat there in this kid's room feeling all at home. Cathy kept brushing her fingers along the top of my head.

'I love shaved hair' she kept saying. 'Are you listening?' I would say. It was very important that she was listening. She was listening. She was pissed too.

'Of course. I'm listening.'

People came and went. Fiona was there running in and waving tinsel. Wrong time of year and all. She thought she was so funny. They said something stupid about tights. Cathy told Fiona to shut the door after her. So of course that meant people knocking and going 'ooh.' But they all fucked away off. Eventually.

'You were saying how you watched your granny die.'

'She just died.'

'God.'

'She just stopped.'

'Och. That's awful.' Her voice was all low. And slow.

'I know.'

'Jesus. But. Like. Jesus.'

And somehow we were kissing. Her hair fell over my face. Someone walked in. I only found out after it was Ciarán.

Cathy giggled.

'Jude you big fruit!'

'What are we like?' I said. But we kissed anyway. And then just sat listening to everyone else being there too.

They were all dull but. I hate them.

'It was bound to happen' she said. Like ages afterwards. When we were slurping tins instead of each other. And wondering what time it was but not being bothered. And what to do next.

'Huh?'

'It was going to happen.'

'Me?'

'Us.'

'Oh.'

'Don't you think so?'

'No.'

'Jude!'

She's such a girl.

'I just feel scared' I said.

'I know' she said. She didn't know. She put one hand on my knee and leant against my shoulder. And went to sleep. 'Worried you might be straight.'

'What?'

'Us' she said.

Us.

What us?

I rubbed my eyes. To stop crying again.

I didn't know what she was talking about. I felt alone. I felt like going home.

'She just died' I said.

'Ssh' she said. 'It's OK.'

I was glad when Mike came in and shook her up.

Cathy got lively for a bit after that. She ended up shifting Mike too. Just to make Mark jealous I think. So then that worked. Mark and Cathy stumbled off together.

Before she left the party quite early she took my jaws in her hands and kissed me lightly. On the nose. 'You're a pet' she said. 'I really love you.' I hugged her. Until she said 'And I had a chat with Mike.' And smiled her evil smile.

I spent the rest of the night avoiding him. The odd time when I couldn't he would be like 'I'm so horny. Where's Shena til I show her?'

I didn't know then why Ciarán was being sulky. I found him in the garden. Playing with a cat. It was licking his DMs and generally being feline.

'Hey' I slurred and he didn't look up. I slumped beside him.

'You smell' he said.

'So do cats' I said. 'Bad' I said.

'I hear you've had your pussy for the night' he said.

He's blunt. I ignored him for a bit but wanted to talk to him too much to bother.

'I'm fucking wrecked' I said.

'You're wasted.'

'Wasted on Cathy' I said. Then shut up cos I didn't know that he knew.

'Yeah. I know' he said. The cat started pawing at his balls so I stroked it too. Just to get close.

'Ow!' he said and the cat jumped back. 'Claws.'

'I'll kiss it better' I said but he just laughed. The cat fucked off but at least. Just us dogs left.

'Cathy shifted Mike' I said.

'Oh.'

'And Mark.'

'Oh.'

'They've gone home.'

'Oh. Oh who cares.'

So I shut up for a bit. But couldn't.

'Shift anyone?'

'There's nobody good.'

He sounded ratty.

'It's cold.'

'We're outside dickhead.'

'Oh. That'd be it.'

'Yes.'

The garden shone because of the lights from the house. Big shadow heads bobbed about. Siamese shadows. A couple of trees were stark enough to be skeletons.

'I hate it here' Ciarán said.

I didn't know where he meant.

'Will we go inside?' I felt awkward.

'I'm going home' Ciarán said. Then he did. I suppose. I stayed in the garden as he scrabbled up and left me hiccuping to myself. And the cat that was hiding in the hedge.

There was no avoiding Mike because he came outside to find me. He made me stand up straight. As if I couldn't make it back indoors. He talked a lot. He was drunk. It was mostly rubbish about some asshole and his acoustic folk rock ranty shit.

I mean he played guitar then. All earnest. Party over.

Good.

'You can't phone your dad in that state.'

'I'm fucking fine.'

'You're fucking dead.'

I mean I was being belligerent. We both were. Me and Mike. As the couples stepped over the bodies and faders and laughed. Or just stayed quiet. But eventually were gone.

'You should crash here.'

'It's not your house fuck's sake.'

'Just stay Jude' Anto said. Picking up a bottle. And rubbing the carpet with his sleeve. He soon gave up.

'Everybody else is anyway' he said. 'Fuck.' Then he crumpled up in a corner of the hall.

'Where are you?' I said.

'What?'

'Staying?'

Mike shrugged. 'Might be a free room' he said.

'I'm phoning home' I said.

'Suit yourself' Mike said. And started to undress. He dropped his tracksuit top on Anto. Bad move. Anto was already dribbling.

He was topless by the time I dialled home. Showing off. He sat in a chair backwards. With a pint of water. The rest of the house was dead. Except for snoring.

'Mum?'

'Oh! Jude! Hello! How are you?'

'Fine where's Dad?'

'Well now hang on did you get the project done?' She didn't sound right.

'Yeah fine is Dad there?'

'No.'

'I need a lift home.'

'Well now it's nearly four in the morning –'

'Were you waiting up?'

'For Dad' she said.

'Where's Dad?'

'I don't know.'

'Pub?'

I caught Mike's eye. He didn't look away. I could see my

reflection in the kitchen window. Zombie. He must have guessed what was wrong. Not hard.

'I might have to stay' I told him.

'Jude?' Mum sounded anxious. 'He'll be in no fit state to drive.'

'I'll stay over.'

'I mean in the morning.'

'You can pick me up.'

'Really?' And her voice took on that tone. Like she would snap. 'Am I meant to wait again for you to call me?'

Mike poured the water over his head. Scrunching up his face and his hair went slick. And started to drip onto his chest. He was doing it on purpose.

'What? No. Yes.'

'Am I meant to run around collecting every drunken fool?'

Fool?

'You sound angry. Chill.'

Mike snorted and flexed.

Cool.

'I don't have time for this' Mum said. Getting tearful.

'Fill in time' I said. 'Have sex or something.'

Mike went bug-eyed and started to gag. In disbelief.

'What are you on?' Mum said sharply. I mean I couldn't help laughing.

I mean what am I on?

Heat!

'Bye!' I said. And tried to hang up. But the receiver fell and she must have heard us collapsing in laughter at our own wit and stupidity. Before the phone began to whine. Forlornly.

'You're such a bastard' Mike said. In admiration.

'You're all wet' I said.

He rubbed his chest hair around a bit.

'You shift Cathy?' he asked. Standing up. Making puddles.

'Yeah.'

I was tired. I switched off the light. We turned blue.

'Me too' he whispered. 'Which means I got you in my system.'

He stepped closer. Nearly knocking over the chair. It scraped against the floor. His face met mine.

'Uh – ' I said.

He leaned against the kitchen door behind me. It clunked shut.

'Just because I talk about other people doesn't mean I don't fancy you.'

I was paralyzed. His eyes were swimming. But he half smiled.

'Oh.'

'For fuck's sake. Just kiss me.'

We fell to the floor. I guess I didn't say no. I suppose if the rest weren't comatose they'd have witnessed the scandal.

We jogged up to Anto's brother's bedroom. Which we were sure was empty. Mike snuck his head round the door and pulled me through. Pressed me up against the wall. We clung to each other til we gasped again for breath.

I grabbed at his wrists. We struggled to the floor. I stuck my knee in his mad hard dick. Cos it made him want me more. He felt strong but wasn't. He moaned a bit. As I bit at his neck. When I let him go he sprang back. And wiped his face.

'Come and play with me' he said crawling backwards. Into bed.

I started off by tugging off his keks. He slipped off my clothes and we wrestled naked. Messing up the sheets. It felt great locking ourselves in knots. Breaking free. The twisting up again and shifting. Being hot and cold and loaded all at once.

I was on top. I brought my knees up to his armpits. Rubbing my arse into his chest. He looked so dazed. He grabbed my cock til it hurt and sucked. Drawing my skin into his mouth and dragging his teeth until I forced my face into his. And kissed him in the lips.

We fingered. And plucked and stroked. It was choppy and hard. It never felt right. It felt good but it never felt right. We didn't care. We weren't letting go til we got some spunk.

'Why do you want to hurt me?' he asked.

Cos you're not him I felt like saying. But didn't.

We slowed down. Licking. Relaxing. Laughing at ourselves.

'69 me' he said.

'Yuk.'

'Go on.'

I got upside down. And spread my legs. He got to look up my hole for a while. Hope he liked it. I was picking pubes out of my teeth for ages.

I wanted to fuck him up the arse to hurt him good. I wanted him to squeal. I wanted him to know how I didn't even like him.

His skin was red and prickly by the time I finished mashing him to bits.

'Fuck me' he said. Pulling apart his legs. He got up like a dog and pointed his behind in the air.

'Not that' I said. Nearly thinking it was funny. 'Turn around.'

'No. Like this. Come on.'

'From the front' I said grabbing for his dick. And twisting it til he faced me again. He was smiling as I slid my hand up his crack.

'I brought rubbers' he said. 'They're in me jeans.'

He wanked slowly as I fell over looking for the condoms. And got confused in the dark and the mess of clothes. His hips made the bedsprings creak.

When I found them I ripped open the box. Three or four slippery packages fell inbetween us. He bent back his legs and kept on wanking. He rocked the bed. I had to concentrate on the lube. I had to concentrate cos I never did it before. It slid into my fingers. Then I jammed it up his hole. I spread it around and then began to oil my cock as well. I knelt in closer. He eased towards me. Gripping the sheets.

'Get that rubber on.'

'I don't need it.'

'Fuck's sake! I dunno where you've been.'

'Nowhere much' I said and thought a bit. 'Always on the safe side.'

'Put it on' he said.

I rolled on the rubber. It was thick as a glove.

'Extra protection' Mike said. 'You need that with anal sex.'

JUDE

I wanted to know how Mike knew. Most of all I wanted to shag but.

I rammed for ages but couldn't get stuck in.

'You're too big.'

'Spread wider.'

'I want your dick.'

It sounded very stupid even to me. He stretched over and squeezed.

'You're a bit floppy.'

Like I wonder why. I could smell him on my hands. It wasn't cool. I would do it right but.

'Try more lube.'

Which made me think again how he'd been here before.

It worked. I slid inside him and he moaned.

'Be gentle' he said. As I pumped too hard.

'Why?'

'You're hurting me.'

'So what.'

'We better stop.'

I kept on going but couldn't feel a thing. Cos the 'extra protection' meant I couldn't feel a thing.

I drew out and ripped off the condom. Dropped it over the side of the bed. Began to kiss him from the balls up.

I pulled him off dead fast and he made me slow down twice. The third time I kept hammering away til the cum spurted. I licked my fingers clean. I was still horny. But he just rolled over.

'Mike.'

111

'What?'

'Mike.'

'Go to sleep.'

When he fell asleep himself I lay there listening to nothing. There should have been people alive in the house. Instead they were all wasted. Lying in heaps. The room stank of Mike. Now that I noticed.

I couldn't lie beside him all night. Someone would find us in the morning. I didn't want to share that anyway. I grabbed all the clothes I thought were mine. I chucked the wrappers out of the bedroom window. It was cold as fuck outside.

I took my stupid stuff to the bathroom. Turned the light on. Dropped everything in a heap. Watched my hard-on fade in the mirror. Washed a bit. Slowly first. Then scrubbed and scrubbed my fingers with soap to try and wipe away the smell of shit.

I took a shower too but the water was freezing. I fell asleep shivering in the corner of the bathroom. I woke up kind of early in the morning. At least before someone needed to go or anything. I even remembered to put my clothes back on. Before I trundled into the landing.

The light was still gray so I didn't know the time. I didn't have my watch so I didn't know the time. I was reluctant to go see Mike in the room. But then I did.

It's funny when you think of rooms where you end up. The bathroom was nice enough. It wasn't fancy. They had plain tiles on the walls and the carpet tiles were scratchy on your skin. But the bedroom was messy. Maybe just the party. The curtain was half hanging off. There were spills on the carpet. It was all green which was weird I thought. Especially with red football merchandise scattered all over.

Mike was in a heap. One arm trailed on the ground. His fingers spread like a fan. A leg jutting out. The muscles all relaxed. His toes were uncurled. Shoulders bunched up. His face was squashed into the mattress. Mouth open. There was a black puddle of spit around his jaw.

I mean I didn't waste time staring. Didn't want to. I tossed his clothes around. I was looking for my watch. I had to slip my hand under Mike cos it wasn't around. He'd been lying on it all night. I didn't even wake him and it was at his belly. He was sweaty still. And shifted a bit when I slid away.

Someone who I didn't know was waking up downstairs. She was walking around and all. But not awake. She had a bowl of Sugar Puffs and a spoon actually hanging out her mouth. And make-up making rings round her eyes. And still had her skittery dress on from the night before. But crumpled.

'Bye' I said. And she waved bye. I gave Anto a kick on the way out. For being a bastard. He didn't even grunt.

I think I liked the morning being cold. I do a lot of walking for nothing. I walked into town cos I wanted a bus. I didn't want a lift. I wanted the first bus. It was good to walk away from Mike. And go home. I mean I didn't care. It was OK. But I didn't want to see him just then. In front of them all. And be me. I'd be pure red and wouldn't say a word. I mean I don't probably anyway.

I sat for an hour. On the Mall. Waiting for the bus. I was

calm after the walk. At first the only ones around were the army. Then the old women and their shopping trolleys. The tartan ones. Then a few kids who checked out my runners and all.

It was funny. Sitting on the bus with my knees up. And watching everyone waking up. We even passed the Mullaghbawn bus where the ones on it stared at us and we stared back. I mean you wouldn't let on you know them or anything. We just pass and stare.

The bus was where I first met Oisín. We all knew him because he was such a queer. And really angry. I suppose we were even more interested after what his brother did. He wore eyeliner to the funeral. And the age of him. It looked so cool in the middle of all the balaclavas. I think that's when I knew I wanted to be friends with him. Years ago when I saw him on the telly. That time. But whether it was just him being so out of place or the memories of all those murdered people that would keep us apart I don't know.

I felt a bit scuzzy in my stomach. I wanted food but couldn't eat. I came in the door at home and Mum wasn't letting on anything had happened. I mean I wasn't either.

'Your father isn't home' she said. That was all about him. But she looked at me suspiciously when I slumped down at the kitchen table.

'Bad night?' she asked. With her eyes all narrow.

'No.'

'I'll make you some soup.' And that was OK.

She'd heard a story from the breadman and chatted away

when I waited for the soup by examining my fingers.

Barry up the road was playing in the garden. I mean he's handicapped. He's a big fella and he's strong but he's mentally handicapped. By accident. But he was playing in the garden of his huge big house and his mother grows flowers. There's always lots no matter what the season. So when he was playing he picked all the heads of the flowers off. He ruined them. He took them to his mother all pleased to help her out.

I slept nearly all that day. I only woke up because I heard Mum tell Dad that either he could go or she would. The row was so loud that it drowned out Patrick crying. I decided that if I made it through the next few days alive I'd give Ciarán a ring and try to make friends with him.

Mike doesn't talk to me in school much anymore.

OISÍN

Knives, forks, tables and chairs, mirrors, make-up, television – bottled water, P45s, CDs, holidays, garden gates – banks with their borrowing, lending and allowing, overtime, discounts, bargains and clothing, fashionable hair and the right car. None of it is natural, yet it is in these things that the paraphernalienation of our lives occur.

To feed and fornicate, dream and defecate, kill, die and create – these are elemental. It is in creation, of course, that all the trouble begins. This accounts for the stuff – whether physical or imaginary – that overtakes our existence and threatens to crush us with our own need to define who we are with what we buy into.

It is something that we all understand, yet can't quite come to believe.

There are no stories. I don't believe in them and neither should you. They'll just try to make you see the world in terms of cause and effect, motivation and manipulation, make you think things happen for a reason. Then you'll believe in fate, or chance, or karma. When of course things just happen for no reason at all. Perhaps we think we have reasons, but it will, of course, look different tomorrow, when we're sober, or out of love – then we'll accord our actions to what we now choose to believe, to whatever story we are currently constructing around ourselves.

You know, we really don't deserve the capacity of reason; so few of us are willing to take it to its logical conclusion. We are born to die. If we were to be honest about our unimportance, we would just kill ourselves now and get it over with. Why do we torture ourselves with money, or beauty, or revenge? Why do we attach importance to these notions? When it comes down to it, we're all glad to fall so sound asleep that we might as well be dead, but with our dreams as reminders of what we never got to do. If you have the dream, why does it even matter if it happened or not? In retrospect, it will be no less unreal.

But is bothering to kill oneself more offensive than continuing to try to carve out a lifestyle? Is the act of self-destruction an assumption of significance?

As I'm sure that I'm failing to fuck with your mind, I'll just try to get on with things, shall I? Which fuck knows is all that we're doing here anyway.

I've made a list of people whom I like and whom I hate.

People I Like – 1. The girl who takes time to paint her nails. She has patterns all over them, each nail is different, yellow squiggles and blue blobs and red streaks and they're fab. She has two purple streaks in her crinkly orange hair and they're not bad either. 2. The bloke who went tearing up the road, shouting something foreign. He was racing to catch up with someone and landed on him with a big happy shriek. I think we all felt we were allowed to look because he was black. 3. Those eejits at home who were caught sniffing glue in a garage. They sealed up the windows and draughts and passed around the Bostik. I'm glad to know someone has the sense to escape, even if it does mean killing themselves in the process. I think they were ratted on by someone they wouldn't let join them. 4. Our absent friends who leave bits of themselves lying on pavements. I faced the other morning to find a pink plastic stiletto lying dying on the doorstep. Around the corner was a blue pair of Y-fronts.

People I Hate – 1. The refugee woman who wouldn't give me change when I bought her *Big Issues*. She stuck her fingers in a little purse and clinked the change round a bit, then clutched at her scarf and said 'no food, baby, no food', pointing at her son, I suppose, who was looking embarrassed. She plucked out 12p from the purse, as if she didn't know what a 50p was, so I waved her away. I mean, she knew I was pissed off, she was relying on it. 2. The horribly organized twenty-year-olds with mobile phones. I'm thinking of this one girl in particular who swallowed all her morals. When we were given the reading list in a lecture, she took her cathode brain from her DKNY bag and ordered them all from Waterstone's. 3. A priest in our parish who ran off with a married man and caused lots of gossip for a week or so. The man had three children and they're all distraught, predictably enough. Apparently Fr-Whoever-he-is had been reprimanded before for his hands-on approach to healing. The quote of the week had to be 'If it had been a woman at least!' Thank fuck it wasn't the children, more like. In any case, it set the cause back by another century or so.

You know what else? Student parties are so predictable. There are the hardcore deadheads who mosh along to Rage Against The Machine singing 'Fuck you I won't do what you tell me' and you just know they'll all be in the front row of their lectures the next day, quietly becoming accountants and engineers. The lawyers are all terribly sophisticated and have plush faces. They're well bred and have a studied appearance, having carefully thought about what they ought to appear to be.

I was latched onto by someone who was an old friend of Seán's. He talked about his talents and remember-the-time-when – and I don't want to remember, so I sank more whatever I was drinking, sank a little lower on the sofa. What came back to me later was that he knows Neil as well.

You know how it is, I could have drifted for hours. Some self-styled zany personality lectured me on the beauty of speed. He hadn't slept in three days, apparently. Around us, people buzzed like flies, vaguely annoying but so insignificant and boring. So trapped in their own microscopic world that I don't care.

There was the one with silly hair, and another with too much eyeshadow that didn't make up for an absence of personality. I remember two were caught shagging in someone else's bed even though there was a perfectly respectable sleeping-bag in the spare room. That caused a three-second scandal, til the jock couldn't hold his peach schnapps jelly and puked up blood in the down-stairs bathroom.

So Mr Speed liked my drawings, cos suddenly I was drawing, I did a picture of him with his eyeballs hanging out. 'Trippy man!' – and I sniffily informed him that I didn't need drugs to feel fucked-up. It sounded a bit self-righteous even to me, but it's not like anyone would ever know who said what at any time.

Things only happen at a party to distract you from why you're not enjoying yourself. Because no one seems to realize that drinking yourself sick and shifting the most unsuitable people and weeping like a bad opera is not exciting when you're the star of your own private movie and the scenery is falling apart.

So I'm left sitting there while one by one all the party-goers die and fade til the room is left all empty but for me, rotating in a pool of yellow light.

I felt like I might have been menstruating my love away – a sick deep ache without a centre or focus of its own. It had to entrap me so we could die together.

Of course, I ended up shifting someone unsuitable too, you always do, if it's a worthwhile night. Just to remind myself I do exist, I create silly little dramas of my own. It will end up being an event and I'll wonder why does anyone care? Which they won't.

She was some caramel girl doing biological science. That's really all I know. And she dressed like it was good to be poor because she made a point of being unfashionable. That was why I was vaguely impressed. I'd decided I was fabulously ugly, so much so that I was bound to be fascinating. It worked, or something did anyway. She fucked off, of course, and I didn't see her for the rest of the night but I think she fancied the speedhead instead.

I came out to a couple of people there, quite deliberately for all my drunken dopiness. Perhaps the deliberation was just my being pissed.

I don't remember the details. I remember Damien's shirt was too tight for him, it wrinkled round the armpits and he was going 'You mean you're gay?' and I was obviously saying yes, cos he looked all serious and said 'God, I never realized – you know – people I know. I mean, you don't think about it, do you?' which was a bit stupid, cos of course I do, all the time, stop being fucking stupid Damien.

So of course then there are all the questions like how do you know? And who else is? And what blokes do you fancy? And why? And why are you gay? It was like having a conversation with myself.

In the end, Damien said 'Don't worry' and I wondered what he meant. 'I won't tell anyone,' he said.

Cheers.

Some oversized eejit managed to break tiles on the roof, he was very proud of himself. He shifted the girl who had cut her legs shaving. It had clotted on her tights, she thought no one would know cos her tights were spangly but she was wrong.

Damien's mate told me I was unnatural. I threw my beer in his face and stropped off weeping, it seems, til the girl who wasn't drinking and was cleaning up after everyone else in an effort to justify her existence gave me a big hug and said don't worry and take a deep breath and I was OK again.

Looking back, I'll be glad to be unnatural from now on. I can be as unreal as the rest of them.

I don't recall how I fell asleep, draped with the caramel girl's cardigan across my back. I dreamt about Jude that night.

It was the loveliest dream I can ever remember. They have a habit of escaping, leaving only the vaguest of imprints behind. It wasn't sexy or manic. We were just walking and he had his arms around me, that's all. He was going out that night, I remember that. I was trying to work out if I could go, how I could get there too. I remember being driven in the wrong direction. I don't know if he wanted me to be there. I just remember how he didn't mind how we almost held hands.

Instead of pushing me away, he held me close and I know it sounds silly but I woke up glad and hopeful.

I woke in a room choked with beer cans. Some crushed, some ashen, some half-full. Sets of limbs lay sprawled in confusion. Tea was made, and circulated. Half-remembered faces greeted one another as curtains were drawn to admit the morning. Outside, boring normal things continued. Inside, we felt older, less satisfied or settled.

I know this doesn't sound like much. It all seems very long ago. I only want to show you how things seem to go so quickly, and leave such little traces in their wake. None of this matters but it happened and I feel that if I trap it down on paper it could

start to make some sense. But I really can't be bothered to pretend the people there are people whom I'll ever meet again or
ever care.

It's not that I didn't like them. I didn't hate them either. It's
just that altogether they draw familiar patterns, like every other
party that I've been to since I got here. From time to time, they
swap their roles, but all in all they just stay stoned and restless,
remain inconsequential, pass into a pleasant haze of drunken
nights and awkward mornings-after.

Lectures? Well, I didn't go. I stayed at home and felt quite
bored in bed.

That was when the stories about Seán and Neil resurfaced in
my brain. I began to feel quite proud of what Seán had done. I
hadn't ever thought about it quite so much before. But the way
he chose his cause and saw it through, regardless of the danger —
it's more than most of us can claim.

SNAPSHOT

'Ciarán rang', Jude's mother sang.

'Oh, right! I'll call him back,' Jude said, springing back out the door he'd just strolled through.

'Jude!'

'What?' He stopped in the hall but didn't turn round.

'Is Ciarán – I mean he's not –'

'What?'

'I know he isn't – but is he?'

'What?'

'He seems a little –'

Jude let her fumble unsuccessfully for a while, then relieved her with 'Effeminate.'

'Yes! Effeminate. Just a bit, but he's not, you know –'

'No, I don't know. Surprise me.'

Jude's mother hesitated. She wanted to be delicate. 'Peculiar,' she said, eventually.

'Peculiar,' Jude echoed flatly. 'Well, no, he's normal. But if you mean is he gay, then yeah, he is,' stomp stomp up the stairs, his face flushed – his mother calling from the sitting room – 'Jude! Come here!' Frantic, she was.

Taking a deep breath, Jude flicked off the landing light. He composed himself, feeling tension grease up the air. He slowly descended each step, feeling them stretch wider and higher with every slow second. He leaned against the doorjamb as casually as he could without falling over. He stared at his mother's worried face and despised her.

'Yes?'

'Is he – is he a – good friend?' Her mouth began to crumple like a drawstring bag, holding back all the things she really wanted to ask.

'Yes. We're friends. It's normal.'

'Oh Jesus –' gasp, gasp. He could see pity welling up inside her, threatening to burst. It was not attractive. She was going to explode like an egg in a microwave. 'We just want – we just want you to be – happy.'

Then she wept earnestly. A wave of something – remorse or empathy – ripped through him. Like standing in the rain and watching the lorry belt towards you.

'Mum,' he said urgently, 'Mum, we're just friends. He's only sixteen, for fuck's sake.'

'You mean – well would you then? What if he wasn't?'

'Wasn't gay?'

'Gay,' she said, wrinkling up her pink nose. 'What's gay about them? I mean sixteen.'

'Oh fuck. Fuck you – if you have a problem –'

'I don't mind if – well, I mean if he's homosexual then he can't help it,' she said defiantly. 'I'm an open-minded person' – look at her, all curled up crying on the sofa that she got from some catalogue! – 'I have no problem if someone can't help what they are.'

'Well, fuck off, that's so rude.'

'Is it? Is it really? Well, why, seeing you know so much about it?' The words were angry, but the tremor was there, hovering on her lower lip.

Jude thought. 'Because he doesn't want your sympathy.'

'What does he want? Do you know – do you know what he wants?'

'He wants the same as the rest of us!' – shit. 'Mum,' he tried reasonably, 'he's just a kid. And so he's gay, and he's my friend cos he's cool and that's all. OK?'

He could tell she wanted to believe him. He realized he was on the defensive even if everything he said was true. The problem was what he wasn't telling her.

There was hope in her eyes. She sniffed. 'I don't mind, you know,' she said, her voice gone all small.

'There's nothing to worry about,' Jude told her. Hoping that was true too.

'OK,' said his mother, with a bit of a smile. He put his hand on her shoulder, and she went to pat it but he drew it back and turned for the door.

'Jude!'

'What?'

'You've lost weight!'

'Fuck's sake!'

'And don't swear at me!'

'I'm not swearing at you, I'm swearing with you. Hypocrite!' He smiled over his shoulder. She reluctantly laughed. 'But we only worry about you.'

'I know'

'Are you eating properly?'

'No! I live on cocaine and sherbet dips!' he bellowed – exasperation! – and slammed the sitting-room door behind him, an urgent phonecall buzzing in his brain.

They had arranged to meet down by the playpark.

Jude was being brave. The world was waiting for him to mow it down. He'd been through fields and carved tracks in the grass. He'd seen things scatter. Birds, dogs, girls and boys and bikes had run for safety, sort of.

He could feel the metal give beneath his fingers, vibrate and liquidate at his touch.

As the car began to rut in the earth, he felt a surge of something, maybe blood, flood his body. Now was the time to let go, give in to the flow and scrape of crunching gears.

Ciarán bounced beside him with the belt tucked underarm.

'Go faster!'

'Can't.'

'You wanker! You nearly hit the lamp!'

'I was well clear.'

'Well near, y'mean.'

'Fuck!'

'Close!'

'Yeah, we are.'

'Huh?'

'We were.'

'Yeah.'

They spun around a young kid on a trike, left him spluttering in a little cloud of exhaust, cartoon-like.

'You nearly hit the babby!'

'He's only me wee brother.'

The kerb crawled up to greet them, ate some paint from Jude's flank.

'Put on the radio!'

'It's bust.'

Ciarán twisted it into life, as they skidded into silence for a second. The crackle of distortion licked up Sunday service. Ciarán put his boot through the dials and screen.

'Tis now,' he said.

Neil came out of nowhere to ask what they were up to.

Ciarán was quiet, relinquishing bravado. Joyriding was deemed 'antisocial' behaviour by men in black balaclavas like Neil.

'Seen your mate Oisín Grant?' he asked.

Jude was surprised. Too surprised to even deny that Oisín was a friend of his.

'No,' he replied.

'You might see him around again.'

'I'll tell him you were looking.'

'Don't bother. He'll know he's in trouble.'

Ciarán called him a wanker when he'd strolled out of sight, but the conversation kind of ended with that.

They got back down to business and choked the engine, riding the clutch.

They rode around the park til it all went dark. When the dust and dusk had settled they left the wreck behind.

They didn't discuss why Oisín was in trouble.

OISÍN

I'm tired of singers and students who cry about the relentless beauty of a shit life. Pretty notes, a pretty face, it's OK to be sad. Singers, playing anonymity. Students playing poverty. Everybody in Belfast is false, even the nice ones – especially the nice ones. What the fuck do these people have to smile about? Suicidal boys grow beards here and girls claim their individuality on the colour of their nail varnish. Then there are the actors.

The actors here spend their whole amateurish lives together feeling even more superior to each other than they do to the rest of us. They always seem so much littler than life when you meet them in reality. When they laugh at a joke it's a practice laugh. They never stop. Every conversation is a scene. It's like they're scared to be themselves, as if themselves won't fill enough space.

I miss Shena. At least, I miss the idea of her. I was thinking of the time I asked her out on Newry Mall. She was waiting for the bus, pale and beautiful, wrapped up in wool and I was in love with her. I think maybe I'd worked myself up to being in love with her that day, because we'd arranged to meet, go shopping and talking and flirting of course, just because she does those things.

I was telling her how much I loved her by avoiding the issue altogether. I was going 'I think I wanted to say something, but it doesn't matter,' shitty stuff like that, stuff that made it obvious what I was on about, except, being myself, I wouldn't go for it or do anything decisive. And she was all, 'Tell me, tell me, before my bus comes,' with her laugh, and it started to snow, except it turned out to be hailstones, so it's a good job I'm not superstitious.

Did you know they choose astronauts on their inability to understand metaphor? I read that somewhere, it's not my own discovery really, but I suppose everybody's life is second-hand. It only gets filled up with other people's stuff or there'd be nothing to talk about. Anyway, Shena didn't get the hailstone metaphor, so maybe I should send her floating into space. I could keep her there, suspended on the stars, where she could be seen for miles. Light years.

I was left standing on the Mall, watching her wave from the bus window. I turned up my collar and I wanted a cigarette to flick away, before turning my back on Shena in her scarf and in her bus. Newry Mall, where swans and winos and condoms go to die. There was me, getting all metaphorical, but really just getting sore.

That reminds me, my new boots gave me blisters. I cut them up with a knife and was surprised it didn't hurt. The skin underneath that was a fuchsia colour, I don't know if that's healthy. My jeans are stained where the blisters spilled.

My stupid bank sent my cashcard and PIN to the house when I asked them not to. Someone predictably nicked it and my bank account has been drained. I won't know for an age if I'm getting my money back. I don't expect the police to be much use. I should be more upset, I expect, but somehow I feel like it might be deserved. It's my grant money after all, it's a relief not to have to spend it wisely.

I've been practising striking matches and not letting go. I haven't lost any fingernails, but I burnt a few holes in the desk-top. Not holes, as such, but the wood is wounded enough to hold your gaze. It looks as if some knots have developed a cancer.

I saw the most deformed woman walking around yesterday as if nothing was wrong. Her face was – it's too horrible to repeat it in words. But she was well dressed and had nice hair and people stared and I thought she was brave. No doubt she'd find that patronizing, but I swear if I looked like that I'd never leave the house. I'd never leave my head. My head is a nice enough place to visit, wouldn't want to live there. But seeing her made me grateful for being normal-ugly, very selfish but everyone is anyway.

Now that I'm used to seeing beggars on the street – I wish there was a kinder word than beggars – I don't care for them any more. Doesn't matter if they're men, women, pensioners – I mean old – children, sick or well or alcos or pregnant, I'm bored of them all. I want to kick them and tell them to get a bit of dignity. I mean it's all very well in principle to say 'Help these people', and I always did, before, but there's so many that it ceases to be some exceptional unfortunates. It's normal. Loads of people live like this. If there's so fucking many, why don't they all do something, together, instead of splitting up strategically and playing up their dirtiness for sympathy's sake? They fucking disgust me sometimes. I still cry about them when I'm pissed though.

Peter came around with his shiny new boyfriend. They're both superclean. The boyfriend dresses in plastic, he's an ultra-modern non-perishable good. If I was in the mood I'd tell you their story but I'm thinking of me as usual.

Boyfriend chain-smoked as we all discussed world poverty, or maybe not. I think all we said that was of note was who was a babe and who was a brute. We decided that Peter was a babe and I smoked the cigarette butts when they'd gone. My lips are suitably sore. I discovered that if you drop a burning match onto a used one they might stick together.

Between breathing in his second-hand smoke and getting off on his trash, I feel used. I still love Peter but can't compete with a brand-new friend who hasn't heard the trauma yet. I read some poetry that didn't change my life and thought about going home.

I phoned Neil. As it turned out, he'd been trying to find me. That should have worried me more than it did, but all the way home I could only think of Seán. I wanted to ask Neil why Seán died.

We arranged to meet at the phonebox in Cullaville, it was dead handy getting off the bus. He wasn't too late this time. He let me in and grinned, nodding his head in time to the music.

'Got the radio fixed!'

He was way too chirpy.

'Where d'you wanna go?' he asked, but I didn't care. 'Fair enough,' he said. We went speeding off in Blayney direction.

I was quiet and Neil started fiddling with the radio. He found the news station, and he couldn't help but laugh when the latest news of a sniper attack in Crossmaglen came on.

'What d'you think of that, huh?' He sounded jubilant.

'Hey, it's what Seán would have wanted.'

'Yeah, man,' Neil said, but he shot me a sideways glance, slightly ruffled. 'Aw, he was sound, your Seán,' he added, after a minute or so.

'D'you remember him much?'

'Yeah.'

'Like what?'

'Uh. Don't you remember I used to call round to your house?'

'Vaguely.'

'Well, then.'

The roads were bad but Neil was a good driver. He seemed nervous though. I knew I shouldn't have, but I couldn't stifle the laugh when it came.

'What's so funny?'

'Nah.'

'What's so fucking funny?'

'I was just thinking.'

'Of?'

'Ah, Neil. Remember the last time we were together?'

The car screeched to a stop.

'That,' said Neil deliberately, 'is something we should clear up.'

Yeah, I was scared! I came home to talk about Seán, and I find myself stranded with a randy killer in his car – and all I can think of is how his dick is a funny shape. Hilarious.

'OK,' I said, as normal as possible.

'Just – it never happened.'

'Fine.'

'Fine.'

He started up the car again, and swerved back in the direction of Cullaville.

'I have a girlfriend for Chrissake.'

'Exactly.'

'And you shouldn't have told Roo.'

'Well … you must have known I was going to …'

'She has the biggest gob on her.'

'Yeah'

'Anyway,' Neil said slyly, 'it's not like we ever got to finish what we started. Just like your brother!' he added, laughing.

'Leave Seán out of it,' I said.

But he wouldn't.

*

It's hard to keep track of the dead, and what drove them. He reminded me of Seán in the burning car. His legs over his shoulders and his fingers in flames. I held up his head when I smashed in the window. It cut him up, the glass, I was trying to help or maybe just get a closer look and he died in my hands. I held up his face, some of the car smouldering and the seats all melted, like bits of his body, they bubbled together but his eyes flickered. He saw me before he closed them again, I told him he was beautiful, I think, and he was, with a trickle of blood crying from his scorched eyeball.

Maybe he didn't hear me. By the time the ambulance came I'd let his face rest and he'd died. I forgot to turn off his radio, maybe I should have, but I liked it on. It suited the mood, maybe it helped him take his mind off things.

I didn't mind it. I sat at the door, it was a bit crumpled but it warmed my back, and I looked at my feet. There are holes and creases in my boots, my toes got a bit wet because of the fogginess and damp. I listened to 'Firestarter'. It wasn't a bit funny.

I began to feel sorry and felt my face retreat into my head, when your hands grow and your throat aches and yourself is the only thing in the world. The smell was passing. I was glad I was wearing black, which I wear a lot these days. Does Seán wear anything but a smile? It must be easy for him to smile, and he was in my head when I tried to hear that boy breathing. It was better when he didn't and I could get further away inside myself, shuddering and weaker and wondering what I meant to him when he slipped his gaze into mine. Should I have reassured him or could I have saved him or would it be better to let him die alone? You would think you would want some fucking peace, mightn't appreciate someone to kiss you goodbye.

His face had been mostly intact, not like the rest of him. He had straight eyebrows and stubble, a lean look. What do you say when his body has flown in different directions? I concentrated on his face, bruised on the jawline, soft at the temple, a proud nose and good teeth. He really was beautiful, I had to tell him that. I couldn't tell by his expression if he wanted to remember or forget.

Part of the ditch had come in the window. It looked pretty too, maybe because you don't expect it inside the car. The ambulance men had trouble with the body and its various bits and the ones taking the car away had to prise it from the shuck. I heard that bit afterwards, people were telling me and asking me about it all the time. Everybody says the land wants to hold on to its own, but why, when people tear up the countryside with their cars and stuff? That makes me sound old again, harping on the past. But I could see this boy was worth holding on to, I wasn't going to let the land get him like it got Seán.

I mean, it didn't work, of course. I had to walk away, keep on walking, through the fog that made me look invisible. Even though, somehow, Jude was with me. Ready to join me if that's what I wanted. I don't understand how the touch of his hand is all that returns to me day after day.

You lose control of your feet when you walk, they take you where they will. I ended up somewhere cold off a lane but the fog was so thick there was no point trying to go anywhere particular, so I sat down. What's good about walking and drinking is that you stop thinking. Walking is lonelier so it's what I do more.

Dropping out is surprisingly easy to do. Mum and Dad might not have registered yet what I've done. I'm not Seán.

I've been tired, bored and restless. I was acting weird. I know I was acting weird because that's what happens when you're honest with people for a change. Acting is the wrong word because you stop acting altogether.

Are you all right? Janice asked me.

Not really, no. No.

For some reason, I nearly cried then. I played it over and over. Are you all right? Janice asked me – Janice! She doesn't even like me, for a million different reasons that don't even matter. Are you all right? She asks me over and over again and I still catch in my throat every time. As if I'm going to cry, or maybe puke.

You look very detached, Adam says. You know Adam, he's a nice bloke but his politics are up the left. I think he cared.

I feel a bit weird.

Going out tonight?

I'm going home. Pause. I don't want to go home but there's nowhere else.

I should have stayed in Belfast and drawn Jude. I could make his skin ache under my fingers, blue slices of bone, green bleeding into red, corrupt purple. Soft blank eyes and parted lips.

The pencils could never be sharp enough. I pared them, the colour broke. I saw sharpenings fly to the ground like dying birds, like Jude's thoughts. Colours that wouldn't make it to his face.

My legs aren't heavy, just all used. And my feet aren't heavy, just well used. And my hands aren't heavy.

SEÁN

The other day a bomb killed over twenty people. There are hundreds injured. A misleading message sent everyone in the small Northern town running in the direction of the impending explosion.

The victims included Spanish students, on their holidays. A baby died instantly. Mothers were mutilated. Girls out shopping were sent flying in pieces through glass windows.

One girl who'd just won an athletic scholarship lost her leg. Somehow that touched me more deeply than the dead.

I worry about that.

Men too, some men died, but they never get priority on the news, you know?

Everyone agreed it was a tragedy. The sales of tabloids soared. They managed to milk the carnage for a few days.

There's nothing new in the news any more.

A small breakaway group claimed responsibility, which no one seemed to find ironic. Officially, there are less than ten members, which people seemed to agree was a cynical lie to cover for more widespread involvement. As if dozens of people are needed to cause bloody destruction.

Some guy sitting opposite us on the train was reading a full-colour supplement about the murders. We were talking about our unimportant friends. When the guy shook his head and muttered 'bastards', we paused, unsure for a moment whom he meant.

Me and Sarah went to Belfast for the day. She broke a nail climbing over the railings of a park we weren't supposed to enjoy. 'Shit!' she said, and took a nail file from her fancy little handbag. We sat on the swings and I trailed my trainers in the ground as she smoothed out the tip of her finger.

'I'll need false ones for the formal,' Sarah said. I made a rude joke and she leaned over to hit me and we laughed. Her swing wouldn't swing straight for a bit. I got a headstart, swooping over the bushes that blocked our view. I caught flashes of a fish-shop, a man in a hat, a kid on a skateboard falling off a kerb painted red, white and blue.

'I'm catching up!' Sarah sang, but we were swinging out of synch. The bars rattled, the foundations clanging against the concrete that kept us in the ground.

There was no one else there except three wee boys on the slide. One was always scared when he got to the top of the ladder that was shorter than me. The others were impatient and pushed him til he half scrambled down. Once he went head first and Sarah sharply dragged her feet in the dust, holding her breath, waiting for him to fall over the side. He didn't. He kind of got stuck mid-way. She hesitated and I swung higher and higher, making the swings clang only on my side.

The stuck kid unstuck himself but Sarah was bored. She said so. I took a big leap off the swing when it went as high as it would go, and sprawled through the air, to land with a roll and a bruise on my shoulder. All the kids stopped sliding to watch.

'Do it again!' one of them called.

I just waved and we went off holding hands.

We got wolf-whistled by the five-year-olds.

We didn't speak for a stretch, until we were safe, until we left the Protestant area behind and hit the shops.

I knew, of course, that there wouldn't be a bomb or anything like that today. We were safe.

Sarah was the first girl I ever fought for. We were at school together, but we didn't really know each other then. I was quiet when I was eight – it all went wrong much later on.

Although I played football, wasn't academic, all that boy shit, although I was that, I didn't care much for the aggression that was meant to go with it. In my head, I could make whole cities explode, but I wouldn't fight another fella face to face.

The P6s and P7s were all in one classroom together, our school was too small. After the 11+, when the days got hotter with everyone's temper, the teacher would often leave us to fry while she pottered off for a cup of something sweet.

First of all, we'd start to whisper. If she was gone for any length of time, we'd shout. Eventually, somebody would hit someone else, and they'd be given ten slaps when the teacher caught them scrapping. Then they'd have to shake while their palms still ached.

This guy Joe hated me. I used to laugh whenever he got in trouble or did something stupid, which was a lot. The thing was, underneath it all, I kind of admired him. He was crazy. He would jump on top of cupboards and steal boxes of pens for no reason.

So he started picking on me, because I wouldn't speak.

'Oi! Seán! Say "fuck"!'

I sat there with my arms folded, knowing I was going red and everyone was watching me in silence.

Joe hopped out of his seat and strutted over, punching my arm casually.

'Why don't you ever talk?'

I wanted to cry.

'Why are you so good?'

I wanted to rip off his face.

'Leave him alone,' someone said, but I couldn't turn to see who it was. I was stuck like a statue, feeling more and more angry as Joe pushed his ratty little eyes too near to mine.

'Hit me, you sissy bastard!'

What happened next is a bit of a blur. I remember seeing Sarah catch her breath, her hair was red and fell onto her shoulders. I remember Joe throwing his head back and trying to punch. I remember us both falling over desks, scrambling, and me hitting him further and further back against the window.

Everyone was roaring. It was great. I was fit to burst. Joe ran to the back of the class and shouted some stupid stuff, the loser. I picked up the huge black plastic bin and threw it across the screaming millions and rubble and ruins. It walloped off his upstretched arms as the teacher swung open the door.

I was dead.

It all went quiet.

'Um,' she said. 'Seán. Put that bin back. Um. Go back to your seats.'

Oisín was always even quieter than me. I vaguely remember him being born, but only because of how it affected me. Mum was cranky. Dad was busy. I sometimes pinched Oisín's arm when no one was around. I liked the way his face screwed up like a rose.

Everybody thought he was a gorgeous baby. Mum told other mums how smart and bright he was. However much they put him in a playpen full of trucks and soldiers, he always wanted to play with something pretty.

'He's a girl,' I used to say, and Dad would hit me a smack across the back of my legs. Oisín would keep on combing his doll's hair and smile to himself at me being upset.

He had friends at school. They were all girls. He never got used to the notion of football, or fighting, except at home when he'd throw weird tantrums. That was the odd time, just. Most of the time he was quiet as anything.

I wouldn't stick up for him at school. I like to think that was good for him. He never cared what other boys said, the way they teased him. If he was scared of boys, he didn't let it show. He stared them down. He knew they were stupid. He'd dazzle them with his cheek and his charm and his skipping skills. He drew princesses in castles for all the girls who asked.

At home, I would sit at the kitchen table, filling it up with mucky markers and sprawling drawings on the back of corn-flakes packets. I drew hills and mountain landscapes full of stick-men stories. There were tanks and guns and lookout posts, helicopters crashing and people with their heads blown off. I could never understand how Oisín would sit in neat little poses, colouring dresses in pink. His women – he always drew women – balanced on a single line, like a tightrope, that separated earth and sky.

Sometimes I used the bright crayons as well. You could put patches of colour all over a page, and cover the whole lot in black. Then I'd scratch pictures of colourful roadkill.

We sat at opposite ends of our table, wondering what world the other one lived in. Mum would never stick either of our pic-tures up. Dad liked mine a lot, though.

'Play soldiers with Seán,' Dad told Oisín.

Oisín stared. Oisín had a way of staring like he could see right through your head.

'Look,' Dad said, lining up rows of little green plastic victims. 'Seán owns this army. We own this army.'

'Not on my kitchen table!' Mum groaned, but Dad ignored her.

I sat at my end of the table, cannon loaded. Bombs prepared.

'So we attack Seán's army –'

'No!' Oisín yelled. Dad threw up his hands.

'Why not?' I asked, and Oisín lifted his head up from all the ordered rows of army ranks.

'They'll get killed.'

'They're supposed to get killed.'

Oisín was going to cry. He made me so mad!

'It's a war, Oisín! People die! How can you have a war if no one dies?'

'I don't want a war then.'

'Kill them all!' I yelled, and bombed his army. Dad thought that was funny. Oisín concentrated very hard on uprighting all those injured in the blast.

I remember when Oisín came home crying from school. I walked way ahead, but could hear him coming sniffling behind. All through the Square, with the real green soldiers, past the parks and bungalows, sniff, sniff, mewl. I looked back once and he was fisting his eyes. His bag trailed behind, making sad scuffles.

Mum was home, she wasn't working then. Of course she saw something was wrong and made such a fuss she had Oisín all worked up again. He bawled. He roared. I tried to watch TV.

'Turn that off!'

'Why?'

'Don't "why" me! Turn it off.'

So I did, with a pained zombie walk and lots of gurning.

'What happened to your brother?'

'I dunno.'

'What happened to you, Oisín?'

He snivelled. He was curled up to Mum's shoulder, on the squashy sofa that we used to have then.

'Did someone hit you?'

'No one hit him.'

'What then?'

Of course I knew what happened. The whole school knew what happened.

'He got kicked out of the girl's yard,' I told her.

Oisín hated playing with the boys. He refused. He had much better fun chasing girls around. 'Maybe he's just an early developer,' Mum said, but eventually we all turned a blind eye. So did the school, til that evening.

We'd been playing football. Our teams were organized, in their own way, but we tended to overdo it. Anyway, in a fit of temper, I kicked the ball wide and it went sailing into the girls' yard. Forbidden territory.

'Kick it back!' I shouted, but all the pigtails and ringlets looked at this ball like another planet had dropped into their teddy-bears' picnic.

'Oisín! Kick it back!'

He gave me one of his looks. A few people started to notice.

Some others started to snigger.

'Jesus Christ, Oisín, kick the fucking ball!'

Some of his friends tried to urge him on, he looked weird, it must have been like the whole school was waiting to see if he could kick or not.

'I'll get it,' Joe said. I don't think he meant to get one over me or anything. Actually, I think he was being nice. I was having none of it.

'Kick the ball you little queer!'

That kind of woke him up. Everyone laughing, even some of his friends, nervously. He picked up the football, clumsily, it was nearly too big for him to handle. He hadn't a clue what to do next. His best friend Maeve took it off him and drop-kicked it back into play.

The supervisor saw it all happen, from the sidelines. As soon as the drama had dropped, she made it worse. She took Oisín by the arm and physically dragged him into our yard. Jesus, this time the whole school heard and saw it all.

'Come on, Oisín, it's for your own good. From now on,' she said, 'you'll stay here!'

'Why?' he demanded. You could hear the desperate slide in his voice.

'Do you want your own brother calling you names?'

'Don't care.'

'Maybe you should care.'

'But all me friends –'

'Not another word! Play football'

Well he refused that point-blank. And stamped his foot. And wept. And called her a fat monster.

The lads asked him to join in, occasionally, when they were a man short or feeling spiteful. For a week or two, he hung around the corner between the two playgrounds, but none of the girls would hang around all break just to hear him moan. He even made escape plans, once or twice, and managed to snatch some quality time round the back at the bike sheds, with the other girls' dolls. He was grounded, though, to stick it out with us men.

'Oh,' Mum had said, holding him back from her and looking at him, as if for the first time in years.

'It could be the making of him,' she declared, wiping his cheek with her sleeve.

He resigned himself to his fate, in a bit, and paced the length of the yard for half an hour every day at lunch time.

Oisín seemed oblivious to how mad we thought he was.

Joe was an annoyingly good footballer. I had to train and practise for hours at home. It came very easily to Joe. When I was a bit older and more confident, I used to join the others on the Square.

We would play after school, in scrappy mixes of our uniforms and tracksuits. We were towered over by the Barracks, but we barely noticed. The Square is really big for such a small town. I recall it in its rubbly state, before the council or someone did it up. Scuzzy chipshops. Scummy toilets. Dead old clothes-shops owned by eighty-year-olds who hadn't caught sight of outside life for much too long. It was a box of concrete blocks and peeling paint. At the lower end of the Square we have a statue of some fella standing defiantly over an eagle. The inscription's in Irish so no one's ever been able to read it.

One day, as Joe landed a tackle too hard, a truck pulled up between us and the Barracks.

'They're here,' Joe hissed in my ear. My grazes were stinging. I hadn't noticed how play had stopped.

'Over here.'

Joe grabbed my arm and tugged me to behind a pitiful shrub. I remember what happened. Clearly. Slow motion.

The boys. Neil, Davy, Ronan. Grey, and undecided whether or not to watch. Their faces were pinched up like knuckles.

Mickey, who hadn't a clue what was happening. Mouthing about the ball in play. No one could hear, not really. We wavered on the sidelines. I remember Mickey's trousers turning black as the first explosion let rip. I thought he'd been shot. Bleeding. He'd pissed himself, of course, but I didn't find it funny. It was painful. He shrank to half his size, inside his skin.

The truck shuddered. The tarpaulin that shrouded its cargo tattered. Bits of it flapped in the smoke and aftermath. The Barracks took a battering, we couldn't see. Something – heavy – was being launched over the steel shanks. Joe's breath was shallow but he shook beside me. He shivered electricity. Grasping fingers like a spastic.

On the third massive cloud of black noise I became aware of

my self again. My body blossomed in the sudden snow. Beautiful snow that fell in a pitter-patter pattern. In the drains. On roofs. On our shoes and hair. On tarpaulin. Until something smelled like dinner.

And slowly, sickly, as we looked through each other's eyes and saw our own blank reflections, the snow that fell around us assumed human flesh.

'I don't need no Brits to look for my child.' My father turned to face us, fiercely. We paled back against the wall.

'Get your coat,' he said, pleased with himself for making us scared. 'We're going to find him ourselves. Alone,' he added, nodding, as Mum squeaked in protest.

'It's getting dark,' I said warily.

'All the more reason for you to get your coat quickly.'

Mum patted my arm and drew down the sides of her mouth, her own way of silently pleading for me to do what the grizzly old bastard told me to do.

I dragged my feet up the stairs, frowning. Where would the stupid wee wanker have gone?

When I pulled on my ugly rainproof jacket, I kicked the junk around in my brother's room. He was awfully untidy for such a girl, I thought. There were paints that he'd borrowed from school leaking in the middle of the floor. Tons of socks and the bed unmade. He'd left his New Testament – we all got one free when we started Secondary School – lying face-down in the mess. On impulse, I read the passage it was split open at. St Paul dictating what haircuts we should have.

It didn't provide any vital clue as to where Oisín had vanished in the last few hours … unless he'd run off to be a Jesus-loving hairdresser. That would make sense, in a twisted, Oisín way.

I slipped into my parents' room and dialled quickly, not daring to sit down in case Dad came.

'Hello?'

'Hello there. Is Sarah there?'

'Och, how are you, Seán? Bla bla bla bla bla –'

I was too polite to swear down the phone that the search party was leaving to find the faggot runaway.

'Sarah?' Eventually.

'Yes?' she breathed, as if she knew something was wrong.

'Can I meet you tonight?'

'Don't know. When?'

'At eight.'

She giggled. 'It's a bit dark … and you sound urgent.'

'Seán!' Dad yelled. 'Get your arse down here pronto!'

'Shit, OK, the graveyard, at eight.'

'Love you,' she said.

'Yeah,' I said, and fumbled the receiver back into place. Love you love you love you –

'Come on,' Dad said. He was standing gruffly at the open door. 'And if we see anyone, you don't say a word. Right?'

We stepped into semi-darkness, Mum putting on a brave face in case anyone was watching from behind their curtains.

'I'll be back in an hour to see if he's home,' Dad said.

We decided to split up to see if we could find him. Having already exhausted the obvious possibilities – his friends' houses – we thought he might be lying in a ditch somewhere, or someone's shed. Dad would take the town, check the pubs and shops to see if anyone had seen him recently. I said I'd scour the fields, check around Monog and maybe out to Creggan.

'We'll not go that far yet,' Dad said. 'We'll meet at home at eight in case he's home.'

'That only gives us half an hour,' I said quickly.

'Half eight,' Dad said, though he looked suspicious.

'I want to look as far as Creevekeeran,' I added. 'You know, at least up til the Youth Club.'

That seemed to satisfy him. 'Good lad,' he said, clapping me on the shoulder. 'At least one of yous has some sense. Whisht now. Well lads.'

Dad and I stopped at a telephone pole, where three of our mates in balaclavas were nailing up another sign – *Free All Prisoners of Conscience Now!* – with a bad painting of a twelve-year-old boy behind bars.

'Hello Seán,' said a muffled voice. 'Did you get our wee painting done?'

'Nearly finished,' I told him. 'It's going to be good.' Then I traipsed off, crossing the road into a field, leaving Dad behind to do some explaining. I wasn't in the mood to talk to them. There was something in the gloves and balaclavas when it wasn't that dark that I found a bit silly.

I did have a cursory look round the fields. Of course he was-
n't there. I was sure, in so far as I'd thought of it at all, that he
would come back crying in less than an hour, having discovered
that he couldn't walk as far as Dundalk.

I went through Monog, up the Bog Road. There were foundations for two new houses being laid. We'd used the site two
months ago to launch a mortar attack on the Barracks.

I kicked at the kerb and bit my lips, thinking of torn and
camouflaged limbs. Preoccupied, I made my way to the church
– early for a change – for my date with Sarah.

The gates were open and I ambled up the wide steps, automatically assessing the vantage point along the way. There was a clear
view of the flank of the Barracks, with good cover promised by
the old monumental gravestones. Sliding my hand against the
railing that guided us all towards salvation, I came to the door
and let myself push it open. I stepped inside, not sure of what I'd
find, but expectant. There seemed to be echoes straining to break
through barriers of disbelief.

I blew out all the holy candles, just for fun, just to prove to
myself that I didn't care for their sanctimonious glow. I flicked a
glance at the Virgin Mary, whose blank eyes looked right through
me, her mouth an amused half-smile. I suddenly felt very young.

I wondered if a church was protected from bombs – and stub-
bornly shoved the thought to one side.

The mottled glass softened the multicoloured light before I

gently pulled the door open. I allowed myself to focus on the suddenly radiant stained-glass windows. The air felt solid, as if I was trying to swim through the memories of everyone who'd ever walked through this space.

Even the sounds of my shoes on the ground were a trespass. I'd never seen the church so empty. I was used to the indifferent masses, half-spoken prayers, the clumsy organ and thin singing. I was used to the vague shuffle of people who wanted to be elsewhere. I was too used to the distractions of wondering what people were wearing, or trying to pray and look cool at the same time. When the church was flushed of all the stupid, human disharmony, it seemed to know something I didn't.

His black hair shone in the front row of the pews. He was bent in on himself and didn't hear me walking towards him until it was too late to wipe away the tears on his face.

Who was he, this brother of mine, who seemed to cry so easily?

I sat down behind him, feeling as if circumstances were imposing themselves upon us, force-feeding us lines to recite to each other while our thoughts surged in a dozen separate ways.

'Dad's worried.'

'No he isn't.'

'Mum's upset.'

'Is she here?'

'No. No, she's at home. In case you come back.'

'I'm not. I mean I am. I mean I'm not running away or anything.'

'I know.'

He tried to say something else but just kind of hiccupped. I sort of smiled. The sort of smile that's just turning up your lips, trying to close your mouth against all the pity that's about to spew out.

'Why, uh, why? Uh, why are you here?' I tried not to sound too concerned. Oisín knotted his eyebrows and slid his gaze away.

'You don't want to know,' he said, but I suppose I knew already.

We sat in silence. The glare of marble and glass couldn't warm up the cold wooden slats.

'It's in the Bible,' Oisín said out of nowhere. Without turning round, he began to share the little truth that had been festering inside his head. 'It says in the Bible. How if you're worried, you look up this passage in St Paul and he's going on about men and women and their roles and it's not right to, you know, to –'

'I know.' I felt sick inside and I didn't want him to be saying this, didn't want him to be my brother and be saying this.

'To change that,' he said feebly. He was so small and thin for his age. He looked crushed and he was only thirteen.

I nearly puked when I felt the hand on my shoulder. I started, turned to feel her soft hair fall against my face. I instinctively put my arm around her to draw her close to me. She slid into the seat beside me and tickled the back of Oisín's head. His hair was beginning to creep towards that hollow neck, in three little arrows pointing down his back.

'Who cares what St Paul said?' Sarah said sensibly. 'Sure he's dead this years and was a mad thing anyway.' I thought she was talking a bit too loud. I winced at her heavy-handed attempts to mend our broken little boy. 'He used to see things, oh, hallucinations and all. He was probably schizo,' she swept on. Oisín giggled. He half turned. He looked sideways from Sarah to me. Our faces were close, our hands clasped together. As if we were trying to melt into one person.

I loved her so much. I've never felt so pathetically grateful to be allowed to touch someone else before.

Oisín's eyes were narrow as he squirmed out of his seat. He practically tripped over himself just trying to stand up straight.

I could smell Sarah's skin and hear her heart beating. He stumbled off, calling 'Yous'd never understand,' and I hadn't the heart to scold him for being such a teenage sad case.

Neil picked us up. I was in Oisín's room, absentmindedly flicking through his art pad. I was quite impressed, and then a bit ashamed that I hadn't noticed how good he was before. He's still fond of bright colours and has an almost cartoonish sense of design. But in his more spontaneous moments, a darker sensibility has leaked out. He has off-the-cuff doodles of blood, skulls, broken bottles, mad dogs. Twisted birds in twisted trees. He's taken to drawing himself a lot; in various flattering poses, but never shirking from the bewilderment in his own eyes.

He came in to tell me that the ugly bloke was here again. Waiting in the car, with that asshole. I clapped him on the shoulder on the way out the door, but sensed his tension and left without a word. I haven't seen him since.

SEÁN

Neil was in an irritable mood. We had, as it happened, a tricky operation underway. Although I tried not to dwell on the details that I knew, I had spent all day rehearsing my own manoeuvres in my head. I was poised. Internally nervous but externally calm. Feeling physical, tensed up, tight as a noose. I was ready.

'We're not ready,' Joe said over his shoulder, as I hopped in the backseat. He was avoiding looking at Neil, who revved up the engine in reply.

'We're going,' he said.

We stuck to the country lanes, losing ourselves in potholes and ditches. It was only beginning to get dark, and our conversation was limited, flat. I was dying to know what was bothering Joe, but neither he nor Neil brought the subject up. The shards of air that define a row were hovering between them.

We would meet another man who would drive a stolen car. We would transfer the devices from our car to his. I would drive our own car off, while Joe and Neil joined the other man. I didn't know specifically where they were going.

We waited for what must have been too long. Joe became more fidgety. I became aware of an agitated vein in my temple. The oxygen in the car was heavier than us. We were just three men in violet light. The hidden explosives were, I knew, mentally ticking in all our brains. Being rational, we knew we weren't in any danger. But the silence and the dusty ditches played tricks on all our common sense.

'Where the fuck are they?' Neil eventually said. I looked out the window.

'I said, where the fuck are they?'

Joe twitched into life. 'I've got a bad feeling 'bout this,' he said, which didn't answer anyone's questions.

'Really?' Neil said. 'Because that – is interesting.'

I tried to shut off my brain. I closed my eyes, as if the inevitable might never happen if I wasn't there to witness it unravelling.

I've driven alone to Lough Ross. I'm staring through the window screen, which makes me feel more removed from the world. I'm watching the light grow paler and thinner, watching our lives grow smaller. Me and the light could do with a good night's sleep.

I've driven too far to go back.

The squealing, splinters, leakages. I have dried blood underneath my finger-nails and I swear I can smell the semtex packed in this car.

JUDE

It's not that I didn't like being with him. I did. It's just that sometimes people aren't as you expect. I liked being able to walk with
him. And not feel the pressure to talk all the time. We didn't have
to talk to feel we were friends. I think that's usual. With Oisín
it's always what he feels. Or what you think. He's never happy
just to let things happen. You know. If you want them to. Like
natural. He has this need to – qualify everything. As if life was
this big exam. And you have to show your workings-out as you
go along. In case you get the wrong answer. Because then you can
see where you went wrong. That's what he's like. He wants to
know everything. What he doesn't realize is he can't. I know he's
really brainy. And he only has to look at something to understand how it works. You can see that in his drawings. You know.
Of me. Or whatever. Everything fits together so well when he
gets to make up the rules. But then he looks at the real world and
sees everything falling apart all around him. Like how his brother
was killed driving that bomb around. I can understand how he

feels so – you know what I mean. Like he has no control of anything. Random.

It makes me quite angry. For him I mean. Because he could do anything he wanted. And instead he's so worried about putting it all on paper. Instead of doing it. Instead of living. If he could have stopped probing. And questioning. And stopped talking. Then I don't know. Then maybe we could have – in Belfast I mean. He was nice and all. I like him. I really do. But he annoys me cos he won't just let it happen. On its own. As if we don't have any choice. That's the best way. That's the way I want it to be.

With Ciarán it's different. There's a quiet understanding. We just become friends. Without having to go through some big ritual. Like going out on the piss together. Or whatever. I think Oisín was trying too hard to make things normal. Maybe that was for me. Not him. But I was kind of impressed when he was a bit out of the ordinary. He did stand out. People noticed him. I think people notice whether he wants them to or not. It was all I could do to get noticed by him. At the start. And then it was like – too much attention. All at once he wouldn't let go.

Ciarán. He's different. When we have anything to say it's easy. Cos he lets things slide past. He's not so stupid though.

Yesterday he said to me 'Oisín really loves you doesn't he?' And I looked at him. Like I was confused. And then he laughed. As he does. And said 'I mean hates you! Poor Judy!' And gave me such a look. Cos he cuts right through you. He's scary sometimes. He doesn't know when to stop. Chasing me round the lawns. Ducking me in puddles. Having a great time making me feel stupid. He's a laugh. The bastard. He's cool.

Ciarán likes Oisín too. From what he knows of him. He's seen the drawings he's done of me. He was impressed. Though he tried not to let on.

At first I wasn't sure if I should tell Ciarán what my mother said about him. I ended up blurting it out on the phone.

'She said what?'

'She didn't really say –'

'She said I was a queer?' I could hear scorn in his voice. He was nervous too.

'No.'

'She did.'

'Yes.'

'What did you say?'

'I said you weren't' I lied.

'And she thinks we're banging away wha?' Ciarán laughed. He made me laugh too. He was contagious. Except I was worried about Mum or Dad being round the corner. I twisted the cord flex round my fingers. I tried to uncurl it. It wouldn't keep straight. I sprawled on the floor of my parents' room. Dust in the carpet tickled my nose. The hard phone bunched up against my shoulder. My face. It pressed itself into my skull as Ciarán laughed through the speaker. I traced the bones in my face with my unstretched hand. Slowly. I could feel death rising up to underneath the flesh. I imagined the stark empty sockets. And grinning teeth. In that hard square jaw. A skull laughs like it knows something you don't.

'Yeah well thanks for telling me' Ciarán said. He was suddenly abrupt.

I shouldered the phone closer to my cheekbone. I let my gaze slip out of focus. It went all shiny.

'See you round!' he said. And hung up. I lay for a while. I listened to the lisp of the telephone wires slunk from house to house. I didn't feel comfortable. I was spread in the dust. With that phone wrapped around my face.

OISÍN

Getting on the Jobseeker's Allowance is a lot more difficult than dropping out of university. There are more forms to fill in, more people to see, more questions asked, more at stake. I remember how complicated just entering the building was, with turnstiles and dead-ends and a cracked old man in a hut about half the size of him, staring dolefully through bulletproof glass, waiting for me to raid the place – daring me to, really. It was as if they all expected it to happen. I felt uncomfortable, sweaty from the bus journey that they refused to subsidize because my claim might still be rejected. After an hour of dealing with old security men and fresh-faced, blank-eyed younger eejits behind all that inch-thick bureaucratic architecture that couldn't beat their skulls for sheer protection from the outside world, I was issued with new forms, a handbook explaining how to fill them in, another sheet of paper explaining the errors in the handbook. I felt under-standably underwhelmed, and just a little queasy.

Outside, the sun still beamed bright as lemonade but I couldn't help wondering if it showed my face up in all its sudden dependency, anxiety, depression. I felt too young to belong in a queue of desolate income-supplement victims. I felt too young to belong to a potential workforce. I didn't want a job and I didn't want their money. Even if it was mine.

I stared at my own reflection in shop windows, superimposed on high-street fashion, searching for tell-tale traces of how something in me had died. That's a bit stupid, nothing had, but that nothing tugged at the back of my brain, looked over my shoulder, followed me home. It sat behind me on the bus and slapped me across the head all the way home.

I didn't fill in half the questions but they made me when I went back. It was a week to the day later, I was told to send them information on my job applications (we agreed three applications a week was sufficiently zealous to earn my £39.80); I was officially receiving state benefit. Simple.

Two schools of thought on getting the dole are (a) Get all you can out of the bastards, and (b) If you don't consider yourself a patriot, why take the Government's money?

Nobody belongs to group (b) except me.

I got off the bus and walked as far as Creggan graveyard. It's one of those old churches that was taken over by Protestants, the graveyard is full of patriots and poets and it's a bit famous. I bet some of my esteemed ex-college colleagues would lunch on every nuance of its curious ambience, but I find it doesn't move me at all. The building itself is small, grey and more or less what you'd expect. There are some unmarked graves, baldy grass, a mysterious what-might-be-an-older-church whose origins are under debate by people who should really have hobbies. The best bit is the vault where they discovered old bones when some tractor, merrily renovating the sacred ground, fell through the roof. You have to go down these steps they subsequently discovered, and you can look at people's skulls. I find all this much more hilarious than viewing the spiritual resting place of saints and scholars, or whatever the pitch is. What Creggan church, with all its Catholic-Protestant husbandry, does remind me of is how little I care whether you call me Irish or British. You might as well ask if I'm gay or straight. The questions carry all these assumptions that have nothing to do with my life.

To get into the Lawns you squeeze through a decrepit iron fence that used to have a gate, I suppose. There are steps that have eroded and slid into a bumpy path, shaded by a canopy of diseased old trees. A chickenwire fence holds back the overgrowth on the other side. It leads down to a bridge which was once picturesque but is now practical and sturdy. You can throw dead branches into the stream and watch them slip into the future, out the other side of your own private world.

The bridge is only the beginning of a renovation scheme. Reverend someone decided it would be a good idea to launch Creggan graveyard as a tourist attraction. Maybe he's right. After all, there are plenty of English tourists who visit Crossmaglen, poke around the Sinn Féin shop, have their pictures taken grinning beside a bullet hole where some poor bastard died. Perhaps it is less tasteless to have a teashop in the grounds of a graveyard full of poets who are useless to us now.

I have to say I find the Lawns more magical than any lecture on the romantic dead. It's just a loose bunch of spaced-out trees and skeletal bushes, til it extends to a castle on the hill, a madman's house over the edge of a brackened heath, faintly poisonous old ruins of a cottage and stable, where pretty-named illnesses linger in the walls.

You don't have to worry about grades and deadlines, looks and love and being funny, you just have to walk until you've used up all the time you've got and go home happy once again. You can ignore the quantity surveyors who have begun to haunt the place, you can hide from the lads throwing stones in the brook, and if you want to you can just get all mucky in the tunnel underground which me and Seán found once a long time ago. It's lined with moss and your ears start ringing just being there. The Lawns is a beautiful mess, for the minute, somewhere to go and get lost for an hour.

I met a dose of hippies. They were scattered across the middle field, dispersed enough to look like a group who knew they were there to stay. Some were lounging and some were building and others stirred some shit in a huge black cauldron, no messing. Others were just tripping. I was able to wander around for a while without the bother of being spoken to. They ignored my blatant nosiness, all of them in their own little world of love and stew good mother nature. A beard eventually deigned to speak to me, something innocuous about the weather, which was bracing. Apparently. He was friendly enough, I got the impression he'd had a real life til recently. He still understood basic formalities, for instance. Like saying 'hello' and explaining the presence of your drug-drenched commune in a still-idyllic pocket of South Armagh. When he got around to the aim of their scheme, a good half dozen began to chatter and mimic the patterns of friendly speech.

The conservation of Creggan Lawns is their latest scheme. It's a fucking shame about hippies, they mean well and all, but have you ever smelled one? Up close? These ones have started to make tree houses, they live in trees. Funny way to conserve them, you know, sitting around in one and hugging it and all. I swear! They hugged the trees, they communed with nature. I asked them why, and they were very earnest and wanted to educate me about the spirit that every living thing has – mind you, they have funny notions about what being alive even means – and talked about giving the tree back some of the love it had shared with us. I said it sounded like sexual harassment to me, and they looked at me funny, and said it was a gesture of mutual bondage. I thought it was about time to leave – the poor scuts! – but the first guy latched onto my elbow and I had to talk to his foamy big beard for a while. Yuck.

His name was Jackal. Apparently. He wanted to know why I was in the Lawns. Apparently. He liked to talk about himself, but he liked to hear about me too, and how I'd dropped out of university ('Good lad, good lad. You're a wise wee man'), and he told me about how his Dad was dying ('Don't be sad, don't be sad, there's no need for that'). I reckoned he was a queer but he began to explain this pagan rite to me, hand-fasting, like a marriage except there's no church or anything. More bonding. He was going to be hand-fasted soon, he said, to this young woman who was changing her name to Diane, for the moon. Jackals howling at the moon, I said, and he pretended to find that funny. Or maybe he did think it was funny, not much of a life, saving trees.

So he asked me if I had anyone, I said I was single, and he said, no, but do you have anyone, and put his hand on my heart. I didn't mind. And I told him about Jude, well, a bit, the sort of stuff he would like to hear. Like how Jude looks so vacant but isn't, just scared. And how I liked to draw him. The nice stuff.

'So you're gay?' he said, suddenly direct.

'Well, yeah,' I said. 'I mean, you never know who you'll fall in love with next,' I said. 'I could easily fall for a girl – in theory. But, you know. I won't.' He nodded and nodded the whole time.

'What about you?' I said.

'The same, the same, there's no shame in that,' he replied, except he was more talking to himself and scanning the Lawns, a squat, rough figure in a tangled landscape. I wasn't surprised, just surprised that he'd said it. I didn't ask him what about his hand-fasting, or if he wanted to do it, if he was feeling lucky or feeling too old. He must have been fifty. He must have been handsome too, when he was younger, but his face was writ with all the slop-and-mushroom life that was the food of choice for these hippie folk. Years of outdoors had turned his skin to leather. I tried not to feel too sorry for him. We stood for a while, tasting the breeze and watching the birds wallpaper the clouds in a flux of feathers and sharpened beaks. I don't trust them birds. They're ruthless, plucking up worms to swallow them alive, pecking at the runts and timid smaller brethren, squawking out of sight but never far away.

When I awkwardly went to leave he shook my hand with vigour.

'Good lad, good lad,' he said.

'Goodbye, goodbye,' I replied.

'I want to see you here again.'

'Sure! Cheerio!' Get me to fuck out of this place –

'No! Do you understand? I want to see you here again.' He placed great emphasis on every quick word. His face was blank.

I forced a 'yeah' through frozen lips. Half waved. I jumped the tumbling wall, walked all the way to Cross and didn't slow down and didn't look around.

I mean, I could imagine fucking him if I never had to see him again. Just to hurt him, he was a bit of a pity. But I bet a hippy doesn't wipe his bum.

Home looked just the same. The familiar sweep of scrapyard and thorned bushes gave way to the blocks and chunks of mortar and the mortar-bombed. I caught a glimpse of two still figures squatting in the graveyard. Another bus trundled to a halt at the public toilets. I watched the shopping-laden grannies shamble off, then stepped out to the echo of my footfall, breathing in birdsong.

I felt lonely for the first time, being back. I would find my house soon. I hadn't phoned in advance, or told them to expect me. I had duties to complete before I could deal with the rest of our family. Right then, I felt the need to pray.

I watched the church swallow those figures, then wove my way round to Seán's grave.

I marched to Jude's house, which headed the terrace. They were all pebble-dashed, with hopeful windows that gawked all day, imploring visitors to stay awhile, or the noisy kids to keep it down.

The paintwork on the door and windowsills was dispirited and flaked. Because it was an end of row house, there was an extra bit of garden that may well have been roomy enough for a tree, except it had been bricked over. Brave weeds struggled to survive.

I knocked the window that exposed an empty hall. I could hear the clutter before I saw feet descending the stairs, pause, and slowly reveal themselves as Jude's.

He slit the door open, leant against the jamb and pointed his face to mine.

'What do you want?' He was trying to sound sullen, I think. A baby was yapping in the background and trying to play a xylophone with a hammer or something.

'Nothing.'

He looked into my eyes. Didn't draw back the door to let me in.

OISÍN

Clunk, went the baby. 'Stop it, Paddy!' said a woman's voice. The TV flicked through stations, disembodied snatches of entertainment ringing untrue.

'Want to go for a picnic?' I asked.

'You're mental.'

'So?'

'Tell me about your brother,' he said.

'No.'

'Go on.'

Seán used to read gun magazines. They were stacked under his bed like some guys might have porn. He would scan newspapers and laugh. He had fun watching men he'd seen die flash across the TV, hailed as martyrs. He created news.

'One less British bastard,' he would crow.

I never saw the point.

'I've forgotten him,' I said.

He thought a while, scratched his neck, twisted his lips.

'Where?'

'The field, you know, up from the barracks.'

'We'd look a bit stupid.'

'Tonight.'

'You're mental,' he said again, and closed the door. Not unkindly.

I sauntered home, glad to have made the effort. There were girls pushing prams, boys on their wee brothers' bikes, mums with toddlers trailing behind. It was all sort of faceless.

Back in my bedroom, I stuck more disposable art on the

walls. Bags from highstreet chainstores, wrappers in plastic or paper, fragments of shrapnel that I found flung far before cease-fires. These hang suspended. My favourite box is the one for condoms whose use-by date is my nineteenth birthday.

SNAPSHOT

The serenade of vehicles came and went, until at last a vast peace stretched for minutes either way along the bogside road.

Stepping over shadows, two boys broke through hedgerow to stumble, fall and lie still in the stubble of the freshly mown field. Oisín let his hand roam the grass.

'McKenna wouldn't like us being here' Jude said.

'Why not?'

'Cos its his field.'

'He doesn't own it.'

'He does own it.'

'He can't own it.'

'He bought it and he can build a factory on it and make stuff and send it to shops and make money that's the way the world works.'

'Whose world?'

'Whose world?' Jude mocked. 'Can you never just talk about normal stuff?'

What's normal? Oisín wanted to say, but thought better. He scratched a couple of stones together and wondered why they didn't spark.

'Is he really building a factory?'

'Dunno.'

'You never know.'

'He's supposed to.'

'Won't stop me breaking in and smashing all his bottles.'

'What bottles?'

'He's a vet.'

There was silence til the boredom threshold broke.

'Why did you drop out of university?'

'It was shit.' Then, feeling a more adequate justification was needed, 'I didn't go to lectures.'

'Aw.'

Scritch-scratch scritch-scratch digging up the grass. I could dig down low and find some worms.

'Do there be worms in these fields?'

'That's not a reason.'

'Um?'

'That's no reason for dropping out. It's more – part of dropping out.'

'A symptom,' Oisín said. Then there was no talk for a while.

'There's a big question mark in the stars,' Jude said wistfully.

Oisín laughed and turned himself over onto his back, knocking elbows. He automatically drew back, then let it slide into place again. It felt more right.

'It's the plough. The big dipper.'

'I'll big dipper you,' Jude said, lunging on top of him, knocking out his breath. Jude dug Oisín's wrists into the earth, his knees striding wriggling hips.

'Why did you drop out of university?' he asked with a smirk.

'Cos it was too textbooky,' Oisín said slowly.

'More.'

'You don't expect politics to be out of a book -'

'More.'

'And cos you weren't there.'

'Aw, shut up,' Jude said, relinquishing his grasp. Oisín could hear the smile in his voice.

'Hey!' he yelped, suddenly inspired. 'Let's do some graffiti!'

'Y'wha?'

'See that? Let's swap the letters round,' Oisín was pointing to McKenna's silage. It was daubed with the legend UP THE RANGERS.

'I hate football. I really hate Cross Rangers.'

'The bags are too big.'

'There's two of us, dickhead.'

'We could make it UP THE RA!' Jude laughed.

Oisín shot him a long thin look, his mouth turned grim. Jude remembered.

'Sorry.'

'I've got a better idea,' Oisín said lowly.

Scuffle on the black bed – digging and ploughing, grappling for a stranglehold on truth. The air sinks. Walls loom and topple, blindly the boys fight on – shunting and tearing through each other, bursting seams, an ecstasy of fumbling.

In moments they connect – as Jude's breath melts on Oisín's skin, as they taste one another's sweat, as they swallow.

Each new bombshell bears Oisín further into the past. Jude is frantic and wrenches his muscles. Meanwhile, as the future ticks by, they shoot each other full of the bullets of a mutual but mirrored love.

The next morning McKenna was dismayed to find his property vandalized. The remains of a picnic littered his gateway. The fence surrounding his precious silage was trampled down. Worst of all, the rearranged bags that now read UP THE ARSE.

OISÍN

I only slept fitfully, aware of excuses that needed to be made. I blinked in and out of consciousness, letting the minutes linger in a tangle of limbs, the tangible scent of ourselves, the half-light conjuring shadows of the night that hadn't yet passed. Perhaps it never would.

His body was a mess. As the morning rose, it gilded his ribcage. It gleaned the sheen of semen, fell and swelled with his steady breathing.

I couldn't bring myself to touch him again, wake him – as I would have to - and see him, gone. I thought of the stupid things we'd done, and how we'd been wrong, and how we could never recapture the essence of innocence waiting for something to happen.

He stirred, his eyelashes waving to greet me. His lips defied a shy smile, jumped up into a grin. With a moment's hesitation, we crawled to each other, lay splayed in the covers until our skins tingled. Why can't I pause that moment forever? I would love to die slowly, pressed up beside him, like face-to-face photographs folded forever, lay in a book that was left to disintegrate. Then we would never grow old or apart, like clichés, or people who live in the real world. Our own world was somewhere, inside our heads, slowly revolving around my bed.

'I'd better go.'

He was right.

I rolled over, let the boy reclaim normality. Took care on the stairs not to wake up the parents, or mice, or whoever was waiting to catch us.

He kissed me goodbye, once, quick on the cheek. He slipped through the door and I shut it behind him, watching his back as he opened the gate. His socks were in hand til he reached the road, when he carelessly stuffed them into his pockets. His tracksuit was dishevelled. That was something that stayed with me as I curled up in the sanctuary of sheets.

Being awake too early makes me relive trauma.

I remember the time a guy pulled a knife on me and Peter. It was after a Belfast trip, we were coming home and got off in Dundalk. We weren't meant to stay on the train that long, we'd only paid as far as Newry. Guys ahead of us in the queue slipped us their passes when we got into bother with the gripey ticket-master.

We were in good form, dandering around waiting for Peter's parents to collect us at the cinema. We rolled around the fountain and weren't bored with each other, despite our day together.

When we paused for a second for the posters at the Venue, a squirt in a puffy jacket went past. He had one of those humpy walks. Trying to pretend he had shoulders to swing. He asked us for the time as I walked on ahead. Peter stopped and told him, it was something after eight. It wasn't very bright though.

'Gimme all your money.'

'Eek.'

'Come on, Peter. Walk away.' I had my back to them and no intention of giving away my money, or bothering to stand around explaining why, exactly. He was such a wee specimen. The kind of guy you stick notes on his back. When I turned around to see why Peter was still squealing, I saw them dancing hand in hand in a circle.

'Come back or I'll stab your friend.'

'No you won't,' I said dismissively. They were grappling over Peter's plastic bag that had his new leather jacket in it. Second-hand new, that is.

I found I couldn't move. In my head I was going do some-thing but my boring old feet were refusing to leap into action and save the day.

'Do something,' Peter groaned.

'Like what?' I said, Mr Logic-in-a-crisis. 'What should I do?' I was looking for his knife and couldn't see one. Dance, manoeu-vre, scuffle.

'Look, the pub's open. Do you want me to go and ask some-one?' Why was I being so calm? Was I just too scared to move? I had enough time to reject this notion, and realize that the whole scene was too plain dumb to believe in. There was no way Mr Bumfluff was stealing Peter's jacket –

He ran. Let go, legged it.

Peter stood a crumpled victor. He ignored the retreating figure and said, 'Why didn't you help me?'

I just couldn't stop laughing.

Peter, shaken and stirred, wobbled over beside me with a dirty look on his face. 'Standing there like a –' he said.

'That was kind of funny.'

'Oh yeah, funny for you.' His voice was all high and squeaky. 'Funny for you cos you can stand there.'

It was hysterical. I swear.

'Why are you laughing?' he asked, very pissed off. We dithered round the corner, sat on the steps of the cinema. Some old shit was showing. Some old same old shit.

'Right in front of the cinema,' I said quietly.

We replayed the scene in the Hollywood glow.

'He was so short,' I said.

'He was big!'

'Aw, he was puny.'

'He had a knife.'

'There was no knife.'

'Oisín, fuck, he grabbed me.'

'Your bag.'

'Fuck! He had a fucking thing, OK?'

'A fucking what?'

'Yoke. For in science class.'

'Scalpel?'

'No – a – scrapy thing. I dunno what it's called, it's just sharp.'

'Like stabby-sharp?'

'Um. It'd give you a bad scrab.'

I really did laugh. So much, it made me nervous. I wondered how nervous I was.

'Is that nervous laughter? Cos it's not funny.'

'I'm sorry.'

'Yeah, keep on laughing.'

'No,' I said, not laughing. 'I mean I'm sorry for not doing something.'

I don't think I'd ever let anyone down so much. I guess no one had ever relied on me before.

'It's OK.'

'It's not.'

'I mean I understand.'

'Maybe – I was scared.'

'Um,' said Peter, not wanting to go there.

'But I dunno! I wanted to really do something –"

'It was all over so fast.'

'Yeah – and then – in your head it's all slow and you think – I tried to work out a plan?'

'In a split second really.'

'Yeah,' I said. 'I couldn't move.'

'I was fucking scared.'

'You still are scared,' I said slyly.

'Well, fuck. I mean, Dundalk.'

'After all day in Belfast.'

'Aw well, it's god punishing us for that train fare.'

'Cool. Then we got away with it.'

'Hum. My nerves.'

'Do we tell your parents?'

'No! I'd, like, never leave the house again. It's bad enough. You're a bad influence.'

'What?'

'Joke.'

But I wasn't sure it was funny.

The steps were grimy and the parked cars were so forlorn that I threw some stones at them.

When Peter's parents picked us up they asked us all the normal things, like 'Did you have a good day?' and 'Did you spend all your money?'

'Great day,' I said.

'Up to a point.'

'A big pointy point.'

'I bought a jacket,' Peter said quickly.

'Jesus, you're stylish. Was it dear?'

'No. It was second-hand.'

'He fought long and hard for it,' I said.

'Would you shut up, you?' Peter said, throwing me a look. He was trying not to smile at me being silly. The nerves were still at him, I think.

'Life on the cutting edge of fashion,' I said, and Peter had to reach the awkward radio with the tips of his fingers to drown out the giggles that were reeling in the backseat.

'The pair of you!' Peter's mother said. 'What are y'like? What are they like?' she asked daddy Peter.

'I dunno,' he said.

That night, I lay in his spare bed. As our eyes grew accustomed to the dark, I could make out Peter's vague shape huddled under covers, even without my glasses. Drops of rain splattered the window and drew scatter pictures in ethereal silver. Light glittered, exploding into points like a trillion tiny sunflowers, as it does when you can't see properly.

We'd only just come out to each other recently at this stage. I'd told Peter about loving Jude. He'd been suspicious.

'You're only trying to get me to say something.'

'Is there something to say?'

'See!'

A few months later it had all become clear. We'd been talking about classmates, I'd been trying to place one of his and he'd described him. I dunno why, but I said, 'Do you fancy him?' I just know he was willing me to ask him. We know what the other one thinks.

Whether I'd expected it or not, Peter fancied this classmate. He was the sort of boy Peter wanted to be.

'It's the love-stroke-jealousy thing,' he'd said.

Tonight there was an edge in the air. The knife might have had a part to play. It might have been irrelevant but I don't think so. It showed how I wasn't the brave one. Or something. The thing is, I've always needed him. He is less able to admit dependency, but I feel I'm dispensable all the same. The need to know where I stand tends to get me into trouble. Witness Jude.

How do you tell someone how much you love them?

'What are you thinking about?' Peter asked tentatively.

Why is there always another agenda, is what I was really thinking.

'Your funeral.'

'The knife?'

'Yeah.'

'Guilt trip?'

'Deservedly.'

'I don't know. Not really.'

'I would have died.'

'Nah. You would have – would you have cried?'

'Of course! Well – I hope so.'

'You wouldn't,' Peter said, surprising himself. 'Oh god, I know what you'd do!'

It's always strange to hear how you're so predictable. In the half-light, blurred-up bedroom, images evolved in my head.

'You'd have painted it.'

'How?'

'I don't know. Blood.'

'My blood or yours?'

He laughed. I'd been serious.

He was still right, but.

The painting would be one of shadows, flat shapes sucked

into a vortex, dizzy round the edges. I don't have to go there cos nothing happened in the end to force it upon me – but it's there, it has a niche, a picture in my head that is stillborn but vivid.

'We know each other too well,' I said.

'Marriage,' Peter laughed.

We always laugh at the wrong time, but it helps. Means we don't slit our wrists.

I hadn't phoned Jude when his gran died. I wouldn't know what to say. I wondered if he needed me, or anyone, then conveniently forgot the whole incident.

I've started to realize how I let people down.

I tried to imagine how Jude would cope with grief. Somehow I think I would turn to coffee, let it infiltrate my bloodstream and carry me away. Jude would be less inclined to take the easy route out. He would have a need to stand back and wonder what his tears were for, and were they worth it? He would look at the body of someone he loved and analyze the mechanisms of death. Although he lends himself to art sometimes, he is, underneath, a scientist, given to balance, measurement and careful dissection. How could I fall in love with a boy with a calculator heart?

Sometimes I think a familiar friend is all you need to get through love.

I have sculpted Jude. It wasn't as I planned, but nothing ever is. I had a hoard of scrap that I'd stolen at Halloween. I dragged it from the roundabout bonfires, rescued broken radios and dysfunctional furniture so I could remould it into something beautiful.

The bits are lying in the garage. It's like another carnage, seeing the ruins of your plan litter a concrete floor.

I forced myself into it. I used those forced photographs. I should have known it wouldn't spark, there was nothing real for it to spring from. The photos were worse than useless, they were burnt out, negative. It's impossible to work with what you're not in love with. The photos were from a time when I didn't give a fuck. It all showed and they couldn't do. The trash was someone else's. Not mine, and not his and it wouldn't make sense. I threw some interesting shapes together with the odd corners and electronic circuits, but nothing more than abstractions. I couldn't find anything in those pieces that I could call my own. In the end, I kicked over the creation and left it where it lay. It's better like that.

I left the photos in a lazy trail.

I saw his face in various stages – a small smile, or a glum downward slant in his eyebrows, spreading to a bewildered close-up, then the spontaneity of unexpected laughter.

The smell of mould in the garage is the first thing to hit me, mingle in my memories. It can bring me back to my flat, and his funny frozen stance. In one sense, the growth of fungus is decay – it breeds in dank and manky places after all – but still it is a triumph, each spore succeeding in seizing control and multiplying, burrowing deeper into death.

I left those fragments behind in the garage, to gather dust and stagnate, while I waited for another idea to spring to mind.

It came to me while I contemplated dead flowers in my parents' bedroom. While the light is always clean there, slicing up the blue floral patterns that decorate the walls and bedspread, the real carnations or daffodils are always stifled.

I clutched a handful of the wilted stems one day, seeing the heads nod back at me, look shyly to the ground. Apologizing for dying. It made me think of how a block of Oasis might serve better than a slender, well-cut vase. I usually think of Oasis as being for wreaths or tributes, and they are normally ugly things. But when I thought of how easy it would be to slice and mould, I saw that Jude would be easier to carve, not build.

I bought a box of dry Oasis from the florists. I thought about structures for a long time, mapping out Jude's form in squares. He's a solid guy, it wasn't that difficult. Then I reckoned how he should be crouching, not standing. The sculpture took form in my mind. It worked itself out through my fingers.

I found I didn't have to think, my hands took over of their own accord.

I took an old desk and daubed it with the school colours. They ran into one another, dappling the desk in a cracked up orange. I wrote across it, quotations from a soundtrack of fucked-up songs.

The Oasis lent itself easily to carving. I worked it in a fury, the green dust flying and settling in my eyes, on my hair, through all my clothes and deeper in my lungs. I could taste it for days after one inhalation. No one was too pleased to hear that.

'It's cancerous,' Peter said.

'So's your boyfriend,' I told him. I realized there were parallels, but Peter was in the real world.

The shapes were exquisite and sat together well, so I didn't mind a little suicide to ensure a piece that worked. His hands were in flames, twisted up between themselves and blunt enough to be forlorn. His face was etched with misery. His shoulders were thrown round his knees, which made for a cage that he locked himself into. His feet, ever awkward, jutted from under him, too huge and curled to be controlled.

The desk squatted over him, torturous graffiti singing his pain. I sprayed him silver, for magic, and was glad to have him trapped in perfection.

My mother was stern but determined to be fair. I saw her grave face concentrated on the kitchen window and knew we were in for a rough few minutes. I put the kettle on in preparation, it was nearly empty. I stood by the sink and waited for our little drama to begin.

'Did you sleep well last night?'

'What?' I wasn't incredulous on purpose, it just happened.

'I had an awful headache last night,' she said.

'So?'

'Now I'm not normally ill.'

'Must have been your hormones.'

'Don't be childish. It's *your* hormones I think we should talk about.'

Click. I turned my back on her to make some coffee. A little landslide of granules, dissolving.

'Are you listening to me?'

'Well, I don't have much choice. I'm three foot away.'

'Don't be sarcastic.'

'That wasn't sarcasm. That was the truth.'

'Don't be clever.'

'Don't be stupid!'

'Oisín!' she screeched, turning white.

'What?' I sipped the coffee, it was too hot.

'I believe you know exactly why we need to talk.'

'Actually, I don't think so. We don't really have a lot to say.'

Her eyes were watching the cats out the back. One was rubbing itself against the window. Another was licking itself clean. Looked filthy to me. Cats aren't trustworthy. They don't give you the dumb affection of other household pets. I read somewhere that they congregate round negative energy.

'Oisín, I know you've had a difficult time of it recently.'

'Really?'

'Well, you dropped out of university –' she said sharply, 'much against our wishes.'

'I never noticed.'

'And you've been moody, but that's understandable,' she swept on. 'No one's had it easy since –'

'Mum.' She stopped. 'Don't.'

I swear I saw a trace of triumph in her face. Like she'd solved me, or something.

'As well as that, there's the dole. We know it isn't easy for you.'

'I'm OK.'

'Though I'm sure you could make more of an effort.'

'Really?'

'Well, there's no need to look so glum. You could get a hair-cut for one. Smarten yourself up a bit.'

How many times had I heard this? I held the cup under a gush of tapwater. It always tastes too chlorinated.

'And then there's the other,' my mother said under her breath. I waited for her to continue, made faces at the cats on the windowsill.

'We've put up with a lot from you!' she said, suddenly angry. When would she get to the point? Was she working herself up to the truth?

'All that rubbish on your walls –'

'Disposable art.'

'– and those obscene drawings you're so fond of.'

I choked. 'Excuse me?' It was difficult to sound convincing. 'What the fuck is so obscene?'

'All that blood!' Her lips went thin. 'And that bruising, it's like, as if –'

'What?'

'Like you're fucking sick!'

It wasn't what she'd wanted to say. She'd wanted to say 'Like a car crash' and couldn't bring herself that far. She trembled but stared me out, hard eyes set in accusation.

'I know he stayed here.'

OISÍN

'Who?'

'That little bastard in the pictures.'

Her face was a study of ugly disapproval.

'We could hear you.'

I didn't care.

'You're disgusting.'

Yawn.

'You make me ill,' she said through cracked teeth. She saw there would be no response.

'Why can't you be more like your brother?'

It was her fake dry cough that made me batter my mother. I could have smashed in her dopey, cloyed-up face, I was sick of her being sick. I should have martyred her on the foot of the stairs, but I gave her a quick, stupid push and raised my hands against the backlash. She just bowed her head and scraped her hands in the air, might have caught my shoulder, and the thick fists that made her body collapse sprung without reason and never stopped til she lay like a quivering bag of kittens waiting to be drowned, sobbing, making a puddle in the corner of the hall. I left by the back garden, a hyper body and a slow-motion brain, still hung up for reducing the woman to a slobbery wee wreck. Fuck it, fuck her, fuck him, fuck me. She could lie there like the bruised up pulp she was, I could drop her in the bin tomorrow. Rancid for years, the house would reek in the morning and I won't ever return again ever.

Dad would come home from work, I reflected as I jumped the fence, and find the tearful wee mewl weeping into her tea. If he didn't search the country that instant then I'm safe til tomorrow, and it doesn't matter, I swear to god I swear I'm never going back.

And now, you cringing bastard, are you a real man? Can you take these fields in your stride, a slaphappy jackboot, dumb, and leaking a trail of sweat? Waiting for the birds to peck out your eyes, or the thunder of your dad coming with a brick, or the drum'n'bass adrenalin to pulverize all senses? Stamping up the stubbly grass, crushing worms and waking up the earth. Rolling down the hill and curling up small to land in a spot where black feathers and brown blood smear a safehaven –

Jude's dog squatted in a muddy puddle. He flexed and clenched his claws, willing me to disapprove with eyes that tore through haze and glade, to find mine, wary, watching from a distance.

He made me uneasy. I could see his dog-cock trembling in excitement, brushing the surface of the bike track he was sitting on.

This was the Mucky Lane, shielded from adults for the most part, held together by a maze of make-believe hideouts, secret routes of passage and a healthy dose of apathetic councilmen. It's a health hazard. A scrape from the thorn bush would boil your blood for a week.

Kids made war on either side of the short cut. It led from the semi-detached crescent, which is where Ciarán lives, to the rampant sprawl of tacked-on terraces, the unlovely home of Jude.

All the other kids used to meet here to blow each other's heads off. There were in-fights and strategies, mind games and power struggles. It was all so much smaller than I'd remembered, which made it all the more sad.

The junk was still piling up. Busted telly, rusted pram. We could have spent hours incorporating each one into a big enthusiastic raid on whoever our enemies were this week.

I used to believe that Crossmaglen, the killing fields of tabloid trickery, had never infested my brain. But it's in everything we do, I realized. It's them and us.

Terrier had something in its mouth. His sharp teeth glinted, slimed with saliva and dripping blood. His tail hopped off a tangle of weeds. I stood on a sofa cushion to softly approach him. His ears flattened. My foot sank into springs and I heard one whiz out of joint as I stepped onto earth again.

I could see a dead bird in his jaws. One tooth had sunk into its chest, exposing a delicate ribcage on which some flesh still hung. The bird's head was at an angle that could only make sense to a broken neck.

The world shrunk to the size of a gleam in the eye of a dead thrush poking from the dog's slavering jowls. It didn't remind me of my mother, if that's what you're thinking. But it's another thing that happened.

I went to the Lawns, as if they had the answers. I half-expected to see the hippies there, spreading messages of consolation through the exhaust-tinged greenery.

It seemed as though they'd gone. There was no tang of residual karma to the air. There was only the broken boards set aside for building shelter, and *God Is Love* nailed to a tree. That wasn't very pagan. It may not have been them. I imagine they'd been evicted, thrown to decompose in another lost cause.

I roamed around, thought *fuck it*, sat on the bridge to count traffic. Waved to the people in their toy cars. I'll never drive, I can't believe in it. It seems so silly to dress yourself up in a metal box and speed along roads where you'll never stop.

I thought of the hippies and why they bothered. Water wound around behind my back. I could lean, fall in, wait for it all to come around again.

She hadn't no right to say what she did. Seán has never escaped us, even in death. She always returns to him, sooner or later, and shows why her older son made her more proud.

He's not much better. Dad, I mean. He seldom says anything more than he has to, but has gone more inside himself since Seán was buried. That's when it finally hit him, I think. The coffin was closed, of course, not much was found. The bomb in the backseat did all it should have. Whatever he did wrong, it killed him, the bastard. I loved him and all, but he hadn't a clue. Took what he could in the way of state benefit – loved education, it fuelled his grievances, provided more reasons to passionately hate all the cultural remnants of England that breed here.

He thought he was right and I bet he died happy. I try not to think of him much anymore, but specific memories – best not to let them fester, or else they might – take over.

Mum and Dad were glad that he joined the paramilitaries. I didn't see his joining them as natural or inevitable. I've never been convinced that the deaths will do much good.

But then, nothing is fair in love and war. When has it ever been? But make sure you win. That is, after all, what everybody wants. I thought that when I fell in love I'd leave a lot of death behind. But love isn't pure and shiny. It doesn't make you happy. Love is war.

Just look at Neil. He liked to shoot soldiers in his spare time. An art form it was. Quick and precise. Just like how I would photograph Jude.

Line up the enemy in your sight, wilfully explode it with your trigger finger.

That way, he would stay forever frozen in the eye of the rifle, or the camera; measurable, unchanging, without any more influence. A statistic or soundbite of your own creation, unable to answer back and contradict. What once had perfect authority could be deflated, flattened, stored away.

Neil thought he could do the same to me. Not kill me, as such, but store me away. He had to meet me, in the dark.

I called for an ambulance before he picked me up. I'm not sure what I intended to do … I knew he was no patriot, that he just liked to murder people. Not like Seán. But when he told me that Seán had grown disillusioned and disappeared with a car full of semtex – I still don't know what to believe.

I knew one of us wouldn't survive.

I didn't tell Peter but he might just have guessed. He knew

there was more to it than I let on. That night, I woke him up cos I had to. The patio door of Peter's front porch has butterflies trapped between the panes of glass. I could empathize.

'Can you see the whites of my eyes?' I asked.

I took Jude to where my brother was buried. We shared a can of beer on the proud headstone.

'I remember the funeral,' he said. 'There were proper guns and everything.'

It was a clear afternoon. The town was quiet. A lot of the passion has evaporated.

'This is the place where some soldier was shot from,' I said.

He scuffed some stones. They're the white glassy sort. Seán wouldn't like them.

'Are you ready for your close-up?' I asked. I couldn't help smiling a little.

Jude took a withering flower from the bouquet someone had left. In honour of our family.

He stripped the stem of its paraplegic leaves. He plucked the petals and threw them at me, one by one.

'Confetti,' I said.

'No more photographs,' he replied.